IN TRANSIT
Mavis Gallant

VIKING

VIKING

Published by the Penguin Group
Penguin Books Canada Ltd, 2801 John Street,
Markham, Ontario, Canada L3R 1B4
Penguin Books, 27 Wrights Lane, London W8 5TZ, England
Viking Penguin Inc., 40 West 23rd Street,
New York, New York 10010, USA
Penguin Books Australia Ltd, Ringwood, Victoria, Australia
Penguin Books (NZ) Ltd, 182-190 Wairau Road,
Auckland 10, New Zealand
Penguin Books Ltd, Registered Offices:
Harmondsworth, Middlesex, England

First published 1988

1   3   5   7   9   10   8   6   4   2

Copyright © Mavis Gallant, 1988

The stories in this collection originally appeared in
The New Yorker magazine

Printed and bound in the United States

Canadian Cataloguing in Publication Data

Gallant, Mavis, 1922-
In transit
ISBN 0-670-82169-1
I. Title.
PS8513.A44I5 1988   C813'.54   C87-094859-8
PR9199.3.G348I5 1988

To William Shawn
with affection and gratitude

CONTENTS

BY THE SEA

❖

AT the beginning of the afternoon, just before the luncheon gongs were due to be sounded at the pensions and villas along the cliff, a lull would descend on the beach. It was July; the beach was a baking stretch of shore on the south coast of Spain. At this hour, the sun shone straight overhead. To the west, Gibraltar wavered in heat. The cliffs behind the beach held the warmth of the day and threw it back to the sand. Only the children, protected with sun oil and porous straw hats, seemed not to mind; they paddled in the scummy surf, dug the blistering sands, and communicated in a private language. Heat fell on the bamboo roof of the pavilion and bar. The bar and the tables and the sticky, salty, half-naked tourists were covered alike with zebra stripes of light and shade. Nowhere was cool enough or dark enough. The glasses on the tables were filled to the brim with ice. No one said much.

In the neutral area of tables between the English tourists and the French sat the Tuttlingens, from Stuttgart, and Mrs Owens, who was American. They lived in the same pension, Villa Margate (whose owner, like many of the permanent residents of this corner of Spain, was English), and, being neither English nor French, had drifted together. Mrs Owens watched the beach, where her son, aged five, was busy with bucket and spade. She and the Tuttlingens, bored with one another, wished the luncheon gong would be struck at the Margate, so that they would have an excuse to separate.

"She is an extraordinary woman," Dr Tuttlingen suddenly remarked. "Heat does not bother her. Nothing does."

The others stared, and nodded, agreeing. Mrs Parsters, a white towel draped on her neck like a boa, was coming toward them. She wore her morning costume—a chaste swimming suit made of cretonne, and flopping carpet slippers. Leaving the slippers above the water-line, Mrs Parsters had put one bare foot into the surf. The bathing, she said, was impossible. "It's not that it's warm, and it's not that it's cold. It's all the damned insects and jellyfish, not to mention the orange peelings from the cruise ship that went by this morning."

As far as anyone sitting in the pavilion could tell, Mrs Parsters was speaking only to Bobby, her dog, part of whose ancestry was revealed in a noble spitz tail he wore furled on his back like a Prince of Wales plume. A few of the languid tourists looked over, but it was clear, even to innocent newcomers, unfamiliar with beach protocol, that Mrs Parsters had nothing to say to any of them. She stopped at the pavilion steps and surveyed the scattered children, all of them busy, each child singing or muttering softly to himself.

"You are building neatly," she said to Mrs Owens's little boy. She said it with such positive approval that he stopped and stared at what he was doing, perplexed. "Where is your father?" she asked. She had been wondering this ever since Mrs Owens's arrival.

"Home," said the child, with unnecessary pathos.

"And is he coming here?"

"No." Dismissing her, he began piling sand. "Not ever."

"How easily Americans divorce!" said Mrs Parsters, walking on.

Mrs Owens, who had heard all this, wondered if it was worth the bother of explaining that she was happily married. But she was a little overwhelmed by Mrs Parsters.

"It's so hot" was all that she finally said as Mrs Parsters approached.

Acknowledging this but refusing to be defeated by it, Mrs Parsters looked up and down the pavilion. None of her own friends were about; she would have to settle for the Tuttlingens and Mrs Owens. Mrs Owens was young, anxious and fluffy-haired. She lacked entirely the air of competence Mrs Parsters expected—even demanded—of Americans. She looked, Mrs Parsters thought, as if her husband had been in the habit of leaving her around in strange places. At some point, undoubtedly, he had forgotten to pick her up. Tuttlingen, running to fat at the waist, and with small red veins high on the cheekbones, was a doctor, a profession that had Mrs Parsters's complete approval. As for Frau Tuttlingen, the less said the better. A tart, thought Mrs Parsters, without malice. There was no moral judgment involved; a fact was a fact.

Mrs Owens and Frau Tuttlingen looked up as if her appearance were a heaven-sent diversion. Their conversation—what existed of it—had become hopelessly single-tracked. Dr Tuttlingen was emigrating to the United States in the autumn, and wanted as much information as Mrs Owens could provide. At the beginning, she had been pleased, racking her memory for production and population figures, eager to describe her country, its civil and social institutions. But that was not the kind of information Dr Tuttlingen was after.

"How much do you get for a gram of gold in America?" he said, interrupting her.

"Goodness, I don't know," Mrs Owens said, flustered.

"You mean you don't know what you would get for, say, a plain unworked link bracelet of twenty-two-carat gold, weighing, in all, fifty grams?" It was incredible that she, a citizen, should not know such things.

During these interrogations, Frau Tuttlingen, whose

first name was Heidemarie, combed her long straw-coloured hair and gazed, bored, out to sea. She was much younger than Dr Tuttlingen. "America," she sometimes remarked sadly, as if the name held for her a meaning unconnected with plain link bracelets and grams of gold. She would turn and look at Dr Tuttlingen. It was a long look, full of reproach.

"As far as I am concerned, the Tuttlingens hold no mystery," Mrs Parsters had told Mrs Owens one morning shortly after Mrs Owens's arrival. "Do you know why she gives him those long melting looks? It's because they aren't married, that's why." Mrs Parsters, who had never bestowed on anyone, including the late Mr Parsters, a look that could even remotely be called melting, had sniffed with scorn. "Look at that," she had said, gesturing toward the sea. "Is that the behaviour of a married couple?" It was morning; the water had not yet acquired its midday consistency of soup. Dr Tuttlingen and Heidemarie stood ankle-deep. He held her by the waist and seemed to be saying, "Come, you see, it's not dangerous at all!" When Dr Tuttlingen was not about, Heidemarie managed to swim adequately by herself, even venturing out quite far. On that occasion, however, she squealed and flung her arms around his neck as a warm, salty ripple broke against them on its way to shore. Dr Tuttlingen led her tenderly back to the beach. "Of course they're not married," said Mrs Parsters. "It fairly *shouts!* Damned old goat! But age has nothing to do with it."

Their suspect condition did not, it appeared, render them socially impossible. Mrs Parsters had lived in this tiny English pocket of Spain much too long to be taken aback; over the years, any number of people had turned up in all manner of situations. Often she sat with the Tuttlingens, asking clever leading questions, trying to force them into an equivocal statement, while Mrs Owens, who considered immorality sacred, blushed.

Mrs Parsters now drew up a wicker chair and sat down facing Heidemarie. She inspected, as if from a height, the left side of the pavilion, where it was customary for the French tourists to gather. Usually, they chattered like agitated sea-gulls. They sat close to the railings, the better to harass their young, drank Spanish wine (shuddering and making faces and all but spitting it out), and spent an animated but refreshing holiday reading the Paris papers and comparing their weekly pension bills. But this afternoon the heat had felled them. Mrs Parsters sniffed and said faintly, "Bus conductors." She held the belief that everyone in France, male or female, earned a living driving some kind of vehicle. She had lived in Spain for twenty years, and during the civil war had refused to be interned, evacuated or deported, but after everything was over, she had made a brief foray over the Pyrenees, in search of tea and other comforts. Traffic in Spain was nearly at a halt, and she had returned with the impression that everything in France was racing about on wheels. Now, dismissing the French, who could only be put down to one of God's most baffling whims, she turned her gaze to the right, where the English sat, working crossword puzzles. They were a come-lately lot, she thought, a frightening symptom of what her country had become while her back was turned.

"You might just order me a bottle of mineral water," she said to Dr Tuttlingen, and he did so at once.

It was unusual for Mrs Parsters to favour them with a visit at this hour. Usually she spent the hour or so before lunch in a special corner of the pavilion, playing fierce bridge with a group of cronies, all of whom looked oddly alike. Their beach hats sat level with their eyebrows, and the smoke of their black-market cigarettes from Gibraltar made them squint as they contemplated their hands. Although they spoke of married sons and of nephews involved in distinguished London careers, their immediate affections were expended on yappy little beasts like Mrs Parsters's Bobby who prowled around the bridge table begging for the sugar lodged at the bottom of the gin-and-lime glasses. It was because of the dogs, newcomers were told, that these ladies lived in Spain. They had left England years before because of the climate, had prolonged their absence because of the war, of Labour, of the income tax; now, released from at least two of these excuses, they remembered their dogs and vowed never to return to the British Isles until the brutal six-month quarantine law was altered or removed. The ladies were not about this afternoon; they were organizing a bazaar—a periodic vestigial activity that served no purpose other than the perpetuation of a remembered rite and that bore no relation whatsoever to their life in Spain. Flowers would be donated, knitted mufflers offered and, astoundingly, sold.

Mrs Parsters sipped her mineral water and sighed; this life, with its routine and quiet pleasures, would soon be behind her. She was attached to this English beach-head; here she had survived a husband, two dogs and a war. But, as she said, she had been away too long. "It's either go back now or never," she had told Mrs Owens. "If I wait until I'm really old, I shall be like those wretched Anglo-Indians who end their days poking miserably about some muddy country garden, complaining and catching bronchitis. Besides, I've seen too much here. I've seen too many friends come and go." She did not mention the fact that her decision had been greatly facilitated by the death of a cousin who had left her a house and a small but useful income. Her chief problem in England, she had been told, would be finding a housemaid. Mrs Parsters, anticipating this, had persuaded Carmen, her adolescent Spanish cook, to undertake the journey with her. Not only had Mrs Parsters persuaded Carmen's parents to let her go but she had wangled for her charge a passport and exit visa, had paid the necessary deposit to the Spanish government, and had guaranteed Carmen's support to the satisfaction of Her Majesty's immigration officials. That done, prepared to relax, Mrs Parsters discovered that Carmen was wavering. Sometimes Carmen felt unable to part with her mother; again it was her fiancé. This morning, she had wept in the kitchen and said she could not leave Spain without three large pots of begonias she had raised from cuttings. Mrs Parsters began to suspect that her spadework had been for nothing.

"Life is one sacrifice after another," she said now, imagining that Carmen, and not Heidemarie, sat before her.

"That is true," said Heidemarie. She looked sadly at Dr Tuttlingen and said, as she so often did, "America."

He's not taking you, Mrs Parsters thought, watching Heidemarie. The words flashed into her head, just like that. Past events had proved her intuitions almost infallible. You're not married, and he's not taking you to America. Mrs Parsters began to drum on the table, thinking.

Beside her, Dr Tuttlingen was pursuing his investigation of the American way of life. "What is the cost in America of a pure-white diamond weighing four hundred milligrams?" He looked straight into Mrs Owens's eyes and brought out each word with pedantic care.

"Well, really, that's something I just don't know," Mrs Owens said, gazing helplessly around.

"I have a nephew in South Africa," said Mrs Parsters. "He would know."

Dr Tuttlingen was not at all interested in South Africa. Annoyed at being interrupted, he said, with heavy, sarcastic interest, "Cigarettes are cheap in South Africa, yes?"—a remark intended to put Mrs Parsters in her place.

"*Very* expensive," said Mrs Parsters, drinking mineral water as if the last word on emigration had now been uttered.

Dr Tuttlingen turned back to his cicerone, relentless. "What is the cost in America of one hundred pounds of roasted coffee beans?"

In her distraction, Mrs Owens forgot how to multiply by one hundred. "Oh dear," she said. "Just let me think."

"I know a place where one can have tea for five pesetas," said Mrs Parsters.

"Goodness! Where?" cried Mrs Owens, grateful for the change of subject.

"Unavailable today, I'm afraid. It's being done up for the bazaar. It is run by a girl from Glasgow, for holders of British passports only." She added, graciously, "I believe that she will accept Americans."

"What do you get with this tea?" said Dr Tuttlingen, suspicious but not noticeably offended.

'Tea," said Mrs Parsters, "with a choice of toast or biscuits."

Dr Tuttlingen looked as if he would not have taken the tea, or the talisman passport, as a gift. "I am going to swim now," he announced, rising and patting his stomach. "Hot or cold, rain or shine, exercise before a meal is good for the health." He trotted down to the sea, elbows tucked in.

The three women watched him go. Mrs Owens relaxed. Heidemarie began to comb her hair. She opened a large beach bag of cracked patent leather and drew from it a lipstick and glass. With delicate attention, she gave herself a lilac mouth. She bit the edge of a long red nail and looking at it, mournful.

"What a pretty shade," Mrs Parsters said.

"He doesn't want to take me to America," said Heidemarie. "He said it on the eleventh of July, on the thirteenth of July and again this morning."

"He doesn't, eh?" Mrs Parsters sounded neither triumphant nor surprised. "You haven't managed it very cleverly, have you?"

"No," admitted Heidemarie. She reached down and picked up Bobby and held him on her lap. Her round pink face struggled, as if in the grip of an intolerable emotion. The others waited. At last it came. "I like dogs so much," she said.

"*Do* you?" said Mrs Parsters. "Bobby, of course, is particularly likeable. There are a great many dogs in England."

"I like dogs," said Heidemarie again, hugging Bobby. "And all the animals. I like horses. A horse is intelligent. A horse has some heart. I mean a horse will try to understand."

"In terms of character, no man is the slightest match for a horse," Mrs Parsters agreed.

Mrs Owens, trying hard to follow the strange rabbit paths of this dialogue, turned almost involuntarily at the mention of horses and stared at the bar. Sometimes a half door behind the bar would swing open, revealing an old, whiskery horse belonging to one of the waiters. The horse would gaze at them all, bemused and kindly, greeted from the French side of the pavilion with enthusiastic sea-gull cries of *"Tiens! Tiens! Bonjour, mon coco!"*

Heidemarie released Bobby. She looked as if she might cry.

"Now, then," said Mrs Parsters, drawing toward herself Dr Tuttlingen's empty chair. "You won't help yourself by weeping and mewing. Come and sit here." Obediently, Heidemarie moved over. "You must not take these things so seriously," Mrs Parsters went on. "Time heals everything. Look at Mrs Owens."

Mrs Owens took a deep breath, deciding the time had come to explain, once and for all, that she was not divorced. But, as so frequently happened, by the time she had formulated the sentence, the conversation had moved along.

"I wanted to see New York," said Heidemarie, drooping.

"Perfectly commendable," said Mrs Parsters.

"*He* says I'm better off in Stuttgart."

"Oh, he does, does he?" Mrs Parsters turned to look at the sea, where Dr Tuttlingen, flat on his back, was thrashing briskly away from shore. "The impudence! I'd like to hear him say that to *me*. You want to give that man a surprise. Make a plan of your own. Show him how independent you are."

"Yes," said Heidemarie, biting the lilac tip of the straw in her glass. After a moment, she added, "But I am not."

"Nonsense," said Mrs Parsters. "Don't let me hear such words. Was it for this that foolish women chained themselves to lamp-posts? Snap your fingers in his face. Tell him you can work."

Heidemarie repeated "work" with such melancholy that Mrs Owens was touched. She tried to recall what accomplishments one could expect from a young, unmarried person of Heidemarie's disposition, summoning and dismissing images of her as an airline hostess, a kindergarten teacher and a smiling receptionist. "Can you type?" she asked, wishing to be helpful.

"No, Heidemarie doesn't type," said Mrs Parsters, answering for her. "But I'm certain she can do other things. I'm positive that Heidemarie can cook, and keep house, and market far more economically than my ungrateful Carmen!" Heidemarie nodded, gloomy, at this iteming of her gifts.

"My ungrateful Carmen," said Mrs Parsters, pursuing her own indomitable line of thought. "I said to her this morning, 'It isn't so much a cook I require as an intelligent assistant, with just enough maturity to make her reliable.' A few light duties," Mrs Parster said, looking dreamily out to sea. Suddenly, she seemed to remember they had been discussing Heidemarie. "I have only one piece of advice for you, my dear, and that is leave him before he leaves you. Show him you have a plan of your own."

"I haven't," said Heidemarie.

"I might just think of something," said Mrs Parsters, with a smile.

"We all might," said Mrs Owens kindly. "I might think of something, too." She wondered why this innocent offer should cause Mrs Parsters to look so exasperated.

Farther along the beach, Dr Tuttlingen was pursuing his daily course of exercise, trotting up and down the sands under the blazing sun. He looked determined and inestimably pleased with himself. He trotted over to the pavilion, climbed the steps and drew up to them, panting. "I forgot to ask you," he said to Mrs Owens, who at once looked apprehensive. "What is the average income tax paid by a doctor in a medium-sized city in America?"

"I don't know," said Mrs Owens. "I mean it's not the sort of thing you ask —"

"I expect it's a great deal," said Mrs Parsters.

Dr Tuttlingen began to hop, first on one foot, then on the other. "Water in the ears," he explained. He seemed happy. He sat down and pinched Heidemarie above the elbow. "As long as we don't have to pay too much, eh?" he said. "I don't understand the 'we,'" said Heidemarie, morose. "On July the eleventh, and again on July the thirteenth, and again this morning —"

"Ah," said the doctor, obviously enjoying this. "That

was a joke. Do you think I would leave you all alone in Stuttgart, with all the Americans?"

From the top of the cliff came the quavering note of the luncheon gong at Villa Margate, followed by the clapper bell of the pension next door. On both sides of the pavilion there was a stir, like the wind.

"Oh, well," said Mrs Parsters, watching the beach colony leave like a file of ants. She looked moody. Mrs Owens wondered why.

"Goodbye, everyone," said Heidemarie. Her whole demeanour had changed; she looked at Mrs Owens and Mrs Parsters as if she felt sorry for them.

"Life —" began Mrs Parsters. "Oh, the hell with it." She said to Mrs Owens, "And I expect that you, too, have some concrete plan?"

"Oh, dear, no," said Mrs Owens, distracted, beckoning to her child. "I'm just waiting here for my husband. He's in Gibraltar on business. The fact is, you know, I'm not really divorced, or anything like that. I'm just waiting here. He's going to pick me up."

"I rather expected that," said Mrs Parsters, cheering up. One of her guesses at least, had been nearly right. "Just so long as he doesn't forget you, my dear."

Waiters walked about, listless, collecting glasses, pocketing tips. Nothing moved between the pavilion and the sea. Mrs Parsters, Bobby, Mrs Owens and her child ploughed through sand on their way to the steps that led up from the beach.

IN ITALY

❖

❖

"THE joke of it is," Henry kept saying, "the joke is that there's nothing to leave, nothing at all. No money. Not in any direction. I used up most of the capital years ago. What's left will nicely do my lifetime."

Beaming, expectant, he waited for his wife to share the joke. Stella didn't think it as funny as all that. It was a fine thing to be told, at this stage, that there was no money, that your innocent little child sleeping upstairs had nothing to look forward to but a lifetime of work. She had just been bathing the innocent child. Usually, her evening task consisted only of kissing it good night, for the Mannings were fortunate in their Italian servants, who were efficient, loyal and cheap.

"They don't let Stella lift a finger," Henry always told visitors. "Where can you get that kind of loyalty nowadays, and at such little cost? Not in England, I can tell you."

There had been two babies in the bath. The boy was Stella's; in the midst of less cheerful thoughts, it was still a matter of comfort that she had produced the only boy in the Manning family, the heir. The other baby, a girl, was, Stella supposed, her grandchild. That is, she was Henry's grandchild. It was too much, really, to be expected to consider oneself a grandmother at twenty-six. Stella pulled down her cardigan sleeves, brushing at the wet spots where the babies had splashed. In the presence of Henry's grown daughter, she had been grave and devoted, had knelt on the cold bathroom floor, as if no one, not even the most cheap and loyal of Italian servants, could take a mother's place.

17

Peggy, the daughter, had lounged in the doorway, not offering to help. She looked amused. "Doesn't Max Beerbohm live near here?" she said. "I expect everyone asks that."

"We know no one of that name," said Stella, soberly. "Henry says he came to Italy to meet Italians."

"I see," said Peggy. She shifted from one bony leg to the other, started to say something, changed her mind. She turned the talk to Henry. "How like the poor old boy to think he can go native," she said. "Actually, he chose this part of the coast because it was full of English. They must be doddering, most of them. It must be ghastly for you, at your age."

All Stella retained from this was the feeling that Henry had been criticized. She no more liked having him referred to as "the old boy" than she enjoyed Peggy's repeated references to Stella's youth. She was only ten months younger than her stepdaughter, but Peggy made it sound years. Of course, Peggy looked older, always would. She said of herself, as if the idea pleased her, that she had been born old. The features that were attractive in Henry had been dismayingly caricatured in his child. Peggy was too tall, too thin, her teeth were too large and white. Slumped in the doorway, she looked like a cynical horse.

There were so many things one could retort to Peggy, replies at once cutting and polite; the trouble was, Stella never thought of them in time. Now, embroiled in an unaccustomed labour (dressing her son for the night), she could not give her mind to anything else. She held the baby on her lap, struggling with him and with garments that seemed to have no openings or fastenings.

"Why don't you put it down on something, the infant, I mean," said Peggy. "You'll never manage that way. He's too lively and fat. And mine should be out of the bath. She'll catch pneumonia in this room." She beckoned to Stella's nurse, who, hovering in the passage, had been waiting to pounce.

"My little boy doesn't feel the cold," said Stella, unable to make this sound convincing. She dreaded her own baths here. The bathroom had been converted from something — a ballroom, she often thought. A chandelier in the form of glass roses dropped from the ceiling. The upper half of the walls was brown, except where paint had flaked away to reveal an undercoat of muddy blue. The bathroom grieved Stella more than any other part of the house. She knew that a proper bathroom should be small, steamy, draftless and pale green, but try to convince Henry! The villa was only a rental, and even if they lived in it the rest of their lives, nothing would induce him to put a penny into repairs.

"Be sure that the nursery is warm," said Stella, surrendering the baby to its nurse with exaggerated care, as if it were an egg. "Mrs. Burleigh is worried about the cold."

But it was hopeless. No room could be kept warm. The rest of the house was of a piece with the bathroom, in style and in temperature. The ceilings were blistered and stained with damp; the furnishings ran to beaded lampshades and oil paintings of Calabrian maidens holding baskets of fruit. The marble staircase — a showpiece, Henry said — was a funnel of icy air. There was no heating, other than a fireplace in the dining room and a tiny open stove in the library. Over this stove, much of the year, Stella sat, crouched, reading *Lady* and *Woman's Own*, which her mother sent regularly from England.

Henry never seemed to notice the cold. He spent the mornings in bed writing letters, slept after lunch until five, drank until dinner, and then played bridge with the tattered remnants of the English colony, relics of the golden period called "before the war." "Why don't you do something—knit, for instance," he would tell Stella. "Sitting still slows the blood. That's why you're always shivering and complaining."

"Knitting isn't exercise," she would say, but after delivering an order or an opinion Henry always stopped paying attention.

Stella might have found some reason to move around if Henry hadn't had such definite ideas about getting value for money. She would have enjoyed housework, might even have done a little cooking, but they had inherited a family of servants along with the house. Their wages seemed so low, by English standards, that Henry felt offended and out-of-pocket if his wife so much as emptied an ashtray. Patient, he repeated that this was Italy. Italy explained their whole way of life: it explained the absence of heating and of something to do. It explained the wisteria trellis outside, placed so that no sun could enter the ground-floor rooms. During the summer, when the sudden heat rendered the trellis useful, it was Henry's custom to sublet the house, complete with staff, and move his family to a small flat in London. The flat was borrowed. Henry always managed that.

Although she spent much of the year abroad pining for England and reading English recipes, Stella was a country girl, alarmed and depressed by London. Her summers were nearly as lonely as her long Italian winters, for Henry, having settled her in London with a kindly injunction to go and look at shops, spent his holiday running around England visiting old cronies. He and Stella always returned to Italy after a stay of exactly three months less one day, so that Henry would not be subject to income tax.

"I've organized life for a delightful old age," Henry often said, with a gesture that included his young wife.

At times, a disconcerting thought crept into Stella's waking dreams: Henry was thirty years older than she, and might, presumably, die thirty years sooner. She would be free then, but perhaps too old to enjoy it. He might die a little earlier. He took frightfully good care of himself, with all that rest and those mornings in bed; but then he drank a lot. Did drink prolong or diminish life? Doctors were against it, but Stella knew of several old parties, particularly down here, who flourished on a bottle of brandy a day. A compound of middle-class virtues, she was thoroughly ashamed of this thought. Questioned about her life abroad, she was enthusiastic, praising servants she could neither understand nor direct, food that made her bilious, and a race of people ("so charming and childlike") who seemed to her dangerous and dishonest. Many people in England envied her; it was agreeable to be envied, even for a form of life that didn't exist. Peggy, she knew, envied her more than anyone in the world.

"It's wasted," Peggy had said at Stella's wedding, and Stella had overheard her. "That poor little thing in Italy? She'll be bored and lonely and miserable. It's like giving a fragile and costly toy to a child who would rather have a hammer and bricks." Stella had been too rushed and excited that day to pay much attention, but she had recorded for future scrutiny that Peggy was a mean, jealous girl.

"We adore Italy," said Stella now, playing her sad, tattered card. What were some of the arguments Henry used? "Servants are so loyal," she said. "Where can you get that loyalty nowadays?"

"I don't know what you mean by loyalty now," said Peggy. "You are much too young to remember loyalty then."

Stella looked depressed. No one ever answered Henry that way. She began, "I only meant—" But if you had to make excuses, where was the triumph?

"I know what you meant," said Peggy, softer. "Only don't catch that awful servant thing from Henry. He's gone sour and grasping, I think. He used to be quite different, when he still believed the world was made for people of his sort. But don't you get that way. There's no reason for it, and you're much too young. It will make you unfit for life anywhere but here, a foreigner in a foreign country with just a shade more money than the natives."

Peggy spoke with a downward drop at the end of each sentence, as if there could be no possible challenge. She was so sure of herself, and yet so plain. That was class, Stella thought, unhappy. She remembered something else she had heard Peggy say: "She's a nice little creature, but so bloody genteel." In Stella's milieu, one did not say "bloody," and one spoke of one's parents with respect. Stella had thought: They're worse than we are. It was the first acknowledgment she had made to the difference between Henry and herself (other than a secret surprise that he had chosen her) and it was also her first criticism. Since then, she had acknowledged it more and more, and, each time, felt a little stronger. She permitted Henry to correct some of the expressions she used—"Christ, Stella," was his usual educative remark—but, inwardly, she had developed a comforting phrase. We may be common, she would think, but we're really much nicer. She felt, in a confused way, that she was morally right where Henry was wrong in any number of instances, and that her being right was solidly based on being, as Peggy had said, so bloody genteel. But it was slow going, and, at this moment, standing in the untidy bathroom with a wet towel in her hand, she looked so downcast, so uncertain, that Peggy said, as nicely as she could, "Hadn't you better go down and cope with Henry? He's out on the terrace having far too many drinks. Besides, Nigel bores him. It's better if one of us is there."

Nigel was Peggy's husband, a plump young man in a blazer.

It was offensive, being ordered about in one's own home this way, having Henry referred to as a grasping old man, almost a drunk. Once again, she failed to think of the correct crushing remark. Nor was there time to worry about it. Stella was anxious to get Henry alone, to place him on her side, if she could, in the tug of war with his daughter. She didn't want to turn him against his own flesh and blood; in Stella's world, that kind of action was said not to bring happiness. She simply wanted him to acknowledge her, in front of the others, mistress of the house and mother of the heir. It seemed simple enough; a casual word would do it, she thought — even a look of pride.

She sped down the stairs and found Henry alone on the dining-room terrace. He was drinking the whiskey Nigel had brought from England and looking with admiration at the giant cacti in the garden. Stella wondered how he could bear to so much as glance in their direction. The garden was another of her grievances. Instead of grass, it grew gravel, raked into geometric patterns by the cook's son, who appeared to have no other occupation. There were the big cactus plants — on which tradesmen scratched their initials to while away the moments between the delivering of bread and the receiving of change — a few irises, and the inevitable geraniums. The first year of her marriage, Stella had rushed at the garden with enthusiasm. Part of her vision of herself as a bride, and a lady, had been in a floppy hat with cutting scissors and dewy, long-stemmed roses. She had planted seeds from England, and bedded out dozens of tender little plants, and buried dozens of bulbs. Nothing had come of it. The seeds rotted in the ground, the bulbs were devoured by rats, the little plants shrivelled and died. She bought *Gardening in Happy Lands* and discovered that the palm trees were taking all the good from the soil. Cut the palms, she had ordered.

She had not been married to Henry long enough then to be out of the notion of herself as a spoiled young thing, cherished and capricious. The cook's son, to whom she had given the order, went straight to Henry. Henry lost his temper. It appeared that the cutting down of a palm was such a complicated undertaking that only a half-wit would have considered it. The trunks would neither burn nor sink. It was illegal to throw them into the sea, because they floated among the fishing nets. They had to be sliced down into bits, hauled away, and dumped on a mountainside somewhere in the back country. It was all very expensive, too; that was the part that seemed to bother Henry most.

"I wanted to make a garden," Stella had said, too numb from his shouting to mention palms again. "Other people have gardens here." She had never been shouted at in her life. Her family, self-made, and with self-made rules of gentility, considered it impolite to call from room to room.

"Other people have gardeners," Henry had said, dropping his tone. "Or, they spend all their time and all of their income trying to create a bit of England on the Mediterranean. You must try to adapt, Stella dear."

She had adapted. *Gardening in Happy Lands* had been donated to the British Library, and nearly forgotten; but she still could not look at the gravel, or the palms, or the hideous cacti, without regret.

Nigel had gone to change, Henry said, but changing was only an excuse to go away and restore his shattered composure.

"I told him I'd made my will entirely in favour of the boy," he told Stella, chuckling. "Only there won't be anything to leave. They can worry and stew until I'm dead. Then they'll see the joke."

Henry had begun hinting at this, his latest piece of humour, a fortnight before, with the arrival of Peggy's letter announcing her visit. Relations between Henry and his daughter had been cool since his marriage. It was no secret that Peggy had never expected him to marry again. She had wanted to keep house for her father and live in Italy. Three months after Stella's wedding, Peggy had married Nigel. (No one ever said that Nigel had married her.) Henry had not been in the least sentimental about Peggy's letter, which Stella considered a proper gesture of reconciliation. Nigel and Peggy were coming about money, he said, cheerful. They wanted to find out about his will, and were hoping he would make over some of his capital to them now. Nigel was fed up with the English climate and with English taxation. However, if they were counting on him to settle their future, they had better forget it. Henry still had a few surprises up his sleeve.

"Thank God for my sense of humour," he said now.

"Henry," said Stella bravely, "I don't think this is funny, and I must know if it's really true."

"It's enormously true and enormously funny." He was tight and looked quite devilish, with his long face, and the thinning hair plastered flat on his skull.

"Not to me," said Stella. She tried again: "You might think of your own innocent child."

"She's quite old enough to think for herself," Henry said.

"Not that child — my child," Stella almost screamed.

"By the time he grows up, the State will be taking care of everyone," Henry said. "I intend to enjoy my old age. Those who come after me can bloody well cope. And stop shrieking. They'll hear."

"What does it matter if they hear?" said Stella. "They think I'm common, anyway. Peggy called me that at our very own wedding. My mother heard her. A common little baggage, my mother heard Peggy say."

Henry's answer was scarcely consoling. He said, "Peggy was drunk. She didn't draw a sober breath from the time I announced my intentions. She read the engagement notice in the *Times*, poor girl."

"Oh, why did you marry me?" Stella wailed.

Henry took her in his arms. That was why he had married her. It was all very well, but Stella hadn't married in order to be buried in an Italian seaside town. And now, having had a son, having put all their noses out of joint by producing an heir, to be told there was no money!

It had not been Stella's ambition to marry money. She had cherished a great reverence for family and background, and she believed, deeply, in happiness, comfort and endless romance. In Henry she thought she had found all these things; middle-aged, father of a daughter Stella's age, he was still a catch. She hadn't married money; the trouble was that during their courtship Henry had seduced her with talk of money. He talked stocks, shares and Rhodesian Electric. He talked South Africa, and how it was the only sound place left for investment in the world. He spoke of the family trust and of how he had broken it years before, and what a good life this had given him. Stella had turned to him her round kitten face, with the faintly stupid kitten eyes, and had listened entranced, picturing Henry with the trust in his hands, breaking it in two.

"I don't believe in all this living on tiny incomes, keeping things intact for the sake of grown children who can earn their own way," he had said. "The next generation won't have anything in any event, the way the world is heading. There won't be anything but drudgery and dreariness. I intend to enjoy myself now. I *have* enjoyed myself. I can seriously say that I do not regret one moment of my life."

Stella had found his predictions about the future only mildly alarming. He was clever and experienced, and such people often frighten one without meaning to. She was glad he intended to enjoy life, and she intended to enjoy it with him. She hadn't dreamed that it would come down to living in an unheated villa in the damp Italian winter. When he continued to speak contemptuously of the next generation and its wretched lot, she had taken it for granted that he meant Peggy, and Peggy's child — never her own.

Nigel and Peggy came onto the terrace, ostentatiously letting the dining-room door slam in order to announce their presence.

"How noisy you are," Henry said to Peggy. "But you always were. I remember — " He poured himself a drink, frowning, presumably remembering. "Stella, I fancy, was a quiet little girl." Something had put her frighteningly out of temper. She paced about the terrace pulling dead leaves off the potted geraniums.

"Oh, damn," she said suddenly, for no reason.

They dined on the terrace, under a light buried in moths.

"How delicious," Peggy said. "Look at the lights on the sea. Those are the fishing boats, Nigel. It's the first sign of good weather."

"I think it's much more comfortable to eat indoors, even if you don't see the boats," Stella said sadly. "Sometimes we sit out here bundled in our overcoats. Henry thinks we must eat out just because it's Italy. So we do it all winter. Then, when it gets warm, there are ants in the bread."

"I suppose there is some stage between too cold and too warm when you enjoy it," Peggy said.

Stella looked at the gravy congealing on her plate and said, "We adore Italy, of course. It's just the question of eating in or out."

"One dreams of it in England," said Nigel. It was the first time he had opened his mouth except to eat or drink. "We think of how lucky you are to be here."

"My people never went in for it at home," said Stella, suddenly broken under Henry's jokes, and homesickness. "Although we had a lovely garden. We had lovely things

—grass. You can't grow grass here. I tried it. I tried primroses and things."

"This extraordinary habit the English have of taking bits of England everywhere they go," said Peggy, jabbing at her plate. Nigel started to say something—something nice, one felt by his expression—and Peggy said, "Shut up, Nigel."

Soon after dinner Stella disappeared. It was some time before any of them noticed, and then it was Peggy who went to look. Stella was in the garden, sitting on a bench between two tree-sized cacti.

"You're not crying, are you?"

"Yes, I am. At least, I was. I'm all right now. I wish I were going home instead of you," Stella said. "I'd give anything. Do you know that there are rats in the palms? Big ones. They jump from tree to tree. Sometimes at night I can even hear them on the roof."

Peggy sat down on a stone. The moon had risen and was so bright it threw their shadows. "They've gone indoors," she said. "Henry's quite tight. I suppose that's one of the problems."

Stella sniffled, hiccuping. "It isn't just that. It's that you don't like me."

"Don't be silly," Peggy said. "Anyway, why should you care? You've got what you wanted." Stella was silent. "I'm not angry with you," Peggy went on. "But I'm so angry with Henry that I can hardly speak to him. As for Nigel, he came upstairs in such a state that I thought we should have to take the next train home. We're furious with Henry and with his cheap, stupid little games. Henry's spent all his money. He spent his father's, my mother's and mine. No one has complained and no one has minded. But why should he talk to Nigel of wills and of inheritance when we all know that he has nothing in the world but you?"

"Me?" said Stella. Astonishment dried her tears. She peered, puffy-eyed, through the moonlight. "I haven't anything."

"Then that was Henry's mistake," said Peggy calmly. "Or, perhaps it was your youth he wanted. As for you, what did you want, Stella? Did you think he was rich? Hadn't anyone else proposed to you — someone your own age?"

"There was a nice man in chemicals," said Stella. "We would have lived in Japan. There was another one, a boy in my father's business, a boy my father had trained."

"Why in the name of God didn't you choose one of them?"

Stella looked at her sodden handkerchief. "When Henry asked me to marry him, my mother said, 'It's better to be an old man's darling than a young man's slave.' And then, it seemed different. I thought it would be fun."

"Oh, Stella."

The lights of the fishing boats blinked and bobbed out at sea. They could hear the fishermen thumping the sides of the boats and shouting in order to wake up the fish.

"I should have been you, and you should have been me," Peggy said. "I love Italy, and I can cope with Henry. He was a good parent, before he went sour. You should have married Nigel — or *a* Nigel."

The crushing immorality of this blanked out Stella's power of speech. It had been suggested that she ought to marry her stepdaughter's husband — something like that. There was something good about being shocked. It placed her. It reaffirmed her sense of being morally right where Henry and his kind were morally wrong. She thought: I am Henry's wife, and I am the mistress of this house.

"I mean," said Peggy, "that sometimes people get dropped in the wrong pockets by mistake."

"Well," said Stella, "that is life. That's the way things are. You don't get dropped, you choose. And then you have to stick to it, that's all. At least, that's what I think."

"Poor little Stella," Peggy said.

AN EMERGENCY CASE

❖

❖

ANY day now, the doctor had said, Oliver would be going home. Oliver had been sitting up for his meals and going down the hospital corridor to the bathroom for more than two weeks. Sometimes a nurse went with him, holding his hand. It wasn't really necessary, he was quite old enough to go alone, but he looked small and defenceless in the oversize bathrobe that didn't belong to him. His left arm was out of its plaster cast. The elbow hurt, and so did one foot, but it seemed to him that he had always been like this. He did not know that he was very pale and that his eyes looked bruised. When people passed him in the corridor and cried *"Pauvre petit!"* he scowled and shied away from their hands.

"C'est un petit Anglais," the nurse with him would say. Often she would add the rest of his story in a low voice. "It's all right," she would say. "He doesn't understand French. Besides, he knows. The doctor has explained."

The hospital was in Geneva; that much Oliver knew. He knew that he was in Geneva, and that he was nearly ready to go home to England, and that they were coming to fetch him any day. The car in which he had been driving with his parents had turned over twice. He knew that the way he knew he was in Geneva; he had heard a nurse telling a maid or someone in the corridor. He did not speak French, but he understood more than they thought he did. His doctor always spoke to him in English. In English he had told Oliver that Oliver's parents were now in Heaven; but Geneva, and going

33

home soon, and the car's having turned over twice were the facts Oliver had retained.

"Your aunt is coming for you on Wednesday," the doctor said. He made his rounds in the morning and usually got to Oliver's room by ten o'clock. Oliver had no clock, and in any case he couldn't tell time, but he knew exactly when everything was going to happen — when they would come to wash him, when they would wheel in the cart with his lunch, and when they would bring the glass of milk after his afternoon sleep. His room was white and contained two beds, one of them empty and half hidden behind a white screen, and two coloured photographs, one on each side of the door. The photographs showed cows at pasture in the Alps, standing in bluebells. On the back of one of the pictures was Oliver's temperature chart; whatever the nurse marked on the chart belonged to Oliver, and he was quite sure that the picture was his and that he would take it home. There was a glass door, hung with white gauze curtains, that opened out to a little balcony. There Oliver was sometimes taken, bundled in blankets, and left in a deck chair. Since there was nothing to see but a bare, sodden garden, he much preferred being inside, in the room he now accepted as home. He preferred it but never said so. He had never once asked for anything.

Oliver's room was called the emergency room; Mme Beatrice, the most talkative of the nurses, had told him that. They kept it for people who came to the hospital unexpectedly, as Oliver had done, but they also used it for ordinary cases when the floors were crowded. Oliver's version of a crowded floor was a linoleum nursery floor covered with little tanks. He stared while Mme Beatrice told him that he had stopped being an emergency case but was still in the emergency room because there was nowhere else for him to go. She said all this, and he seemed to understand. The truth was that he could not imagine anywhere else.

"Your aunt," the doctor said to Oliver. "Your charming aunt, Miss Redfern, will be here on Wednesday. Won't that be jolly?" The doctor was fat and wore horn-rimmed glasses. He was loud and cheerful and friendly and kept telling Oliver that he had two little boys of his own.

"That's not *my* aunt," Oliver said.

"Miss Redfern," the doctor said patiently. They had been repeating this dialogue for days. "Your charming aunt, who came to see you after your accident."

"Nobody came."

"Miss Redfern did. She is called Aunt Catherine."

"Oh, Auntie Cath," said Oliver indifferently. He bent over his drawing. There was a small painted table set over his knees, on which he played with the modelling clay they had given him, cut up magazines and drew airplanes and cats. He drew cats in boots and pullovers, and he drew their toothbrushes and the tubs in which they were bathed at night. When the doctor, pointing to some clumsy, disjointed shape, asked "What is that?" Oliver covered his drawings with his hands. The doctor was curious about the drawings, because he had mistaken the cats' bathtub for a motorcar and thought that Oliver had been drawing the automobile in which his parents were killed.

He asked what kind of automobile it was, and Oliver muttered something.

"What did you say?"

"I said," said Oliver, shouting, "we've got a bigger car than you have at home."

The doctor told the nurses to be watchful and to report anything Oliver said that might indicate he was unquiet or anxious. Oliver was unrewarding. He did not draw, or mention, accidents, his father, or his mother. He spoke of a place called Bedlington Gardens, where everything was bigger, better and cost more than anything in the emergency room. In his personal reckoning, pennies equalled and perhaps surpassed pounds, but he liked the phrase "costs a lot more." The coming of Aunt Catherine did not excite him. "Is she bringing me a present?" he said. When the nurse replied that she didn't know, Oliver lost interest. He was sitting with the bed levered up and pillows at his back. He still had a pain in his back from some injections, but he was used to it. The doctor had come and gone, and had said this time that Aunt Catherine was coming tomorrow. Now that the doctor's visit was over, Oliver knew that nothing else would happen until lunch, and lunch would be vegetable broth and a bit of meat with two vegetables, kept hot over a dish of warm water. The only uncertainty was dessert, which might be pudding or fruit.

Shortly before lunch, the doors swung open — the padded-leather hall door and the white-painted inner door — and two nurses pushed in a rolling stretcher on which lay a sleeping woman. They pushed aside the screen that separated the two beds, and rolled the wagon up beside the empty bed. They tipped the stretcher, and the woman rolled neatly onto the bed. She wore a short white nightgown, and Oliver saw her legs were fat and white and streaked with iodine. She moaned, but the moans sounded as if they were coming from far away, so deeply was she in sleep.

The doors opened again, and an important-looking nurse, the one who wore a cone-shaped hat and always came around with the doctor, looked at the woman and felt the bed, and said something angry-sounding to the nurses. They had neglected to warm the bed. She spoke in French, but Oliver understood. Then the nurse looked over at him and, changing her manner to something more pleasant, said, in English, "So you are leaving us tomorrow?"

"I don't know." He kept on staring at the sleeping woman.

The nurse went out, and the others followed. Oliver sat up a little straighter, then found he could see better by getting up on his knees. The sleeping woman lay on her back, breathing noisily through her mouth. He watched her, motionless, and was still watching when they brought in his lunch.

"Oh!" The waitress seemed shocked, and she put the screen between the two beds, so that Oliver couldn't see.

"Did she have an accident?" he said, but the waitress spoke no English.

He ate his lunch. After a bit, a nurse came in and disappeared behind the screen. "Feeling better?" he heard her say, very loud.

The heavy breathing stopped, and a faraway voice said, "Yes, I'm all right."

He heard a rattling sound, then the nurse's voice again: "Do not swallow, please. Hold the water in your mouth and spit it out."

"Is that mine I hear crying?" said the voice, as if its owner were coming closer to the surface.

"You are hearing them all," said the nurse. "This room is over the nursery. I'm afraid it is the emergency room, and not very comfortable. We really were not expecting you just yet."

"Nearly had her on the plane," said the woman, and Oliver heard her laugh softly. He liked her voice, now that it sounded less buried.

"Did you have an accident?" he said loudly.

"There is a little boy in the room," the nurse said swiftly, "but he goes tomorrow." Her voice dropped and Oliver heard only certain words. He felt the tone, full of anxiety, and he felt the sensation in the room of shared secrets.

"Poor little thing," he heard. "Take the screen away. Can I sit up?"

"Not yet." The screen was folded back, and Oliver and the sick lady looked at each other. She had the expression he had seen on people in the corridor and on the faces of new nurses who had just had everything explained to them.

"So you speak English," she said, at last. "I'm so pleased. I shall have someone to talk to, at least until you go."

"Did you have an accident?" he said again.

The two women laughed together. "Mrs Chapman found a baby in a cabbage in the garden," said the nurse.

Oliver did not reply.

They replaced the screen later in the day, and the nurse told Oliver to be very quiet so that Mrs Chapman could sleep. He did not see her again until the next morning, after his bath. Then they took the screen away, because it was a sunny day and the screen hid the sun from his neighbour. She lay very flat, and Oliver had to kneel on his bed again in order to see her face. She was not young and not pretty.

"That was a nasty dream you had last night, Oliver," she said. "What was it all about?"

"Didn't dream."

"Don't you remember? I rang for the nurse. We put the light on. You spoke to us. Don't you remember at all?"

He said, "I didn't dream. Did finding the baby make you sick?"

She laughed and winced and said, "Don't make me laugh. It hurts. I didn't find the baby. I had it. But that's not what made me sick. I'll tell you all about it if — Can you get out of bed? Of course you can. I saw you trotting off earlier. And you're going home today. Well, then, get out of bed and come over here and find my purse in that drawer. Open the purse and you'll find a packet of cigarettes, and some matches in a little box. Take them out."

He was already across the room, in his white hospital jacket open down the back. The tiles of the floor were cold under his feet. He opened the bag with great care and found the cigarettes and the matches. "You've got money," he said, looking inside, "and a comb, and a dirty handkerchief."

"Don't be rude," said Mrs Chapman. "Throw over the cigarettes. Can you find me an ashtray? What about the saucer under the drinking glass? That's it." He placed the saucer carefully on the white counterpane and stood waiting. She lit the cigarette and held her breath, and then blew out smoke. "Thank God for that," she said. "I enjoy cigarettes again. I never stopped smoking, but I just didn't enjoy it. Now, let me see. What did I start to tell you? Oh, yes. Well, after I had my baby — she's my fifth, so I can nearly think about something else at the same time — about two hours after, I had to have an operation. That's what made me sick. Understand?"

He nodded. "I had an accident," he said.

"I know."

Oliver stirred, waiting. "What else is there?" he said.

"You mean what else about me?"

He wasn't sure what he meant. He didn't want to get back into bed, and he liked watching her while she smoked.

"Do you want to know why I'm in Geneva?" she said. "Because my husband works here. Do you want to know where he is now? He's at a conference in Ceylon. That's so far away I won't even try to tell you about it. Do you want to know why I was on a plane? Because I had to go to

England to see *my* mother. She was ill and in a nursing home just like this. Do you like all that?"

"Yes." They smiled comfortably at each other.

"I expect you ought to be in bed," Mrs Chapman said.

"The doctor comes soon," Oliver said. "The doctor comes, and then lunch."

"You've got the timetable down perfectly," she said. "But I still think you'd better get back into bed."

"My Auntie Cath's coming," he said, lingering.

"She's taking you home, is she?"

"No," said Oliver scornfully, drawing it out. "She can't take me home. We don't even live in the same place."

He climbed back in his bed and watched the door. There was a curious air of change about the day. When the doctor came in, he scarcely looked at Oliver, except to say "Well, my brave little man," which was not his usual manner at all. The waitress who brought the comforting lunch of soup and meat and vegetables said *"Au revoir, mon petit,"* which was quite new. A maid came in and took away the modelling clay. It didn't belong to Oliver but to the hospital. Mrs Chapman slept, not in the moaning way of the day before but quietly. She awoke suddenly and told Oliver that she felt very well indeed.

"Shall I get you a cigarette now?" he said. He had been waiting for this.

"I can reach them, thank you." She looked across at him and said, "You can't read yet, can you?"

"I've got books."

"I know. I mean, can you read writing?...I thought not. Don't be so offended. I'm going to write down my address and my name, and maybe your aunt will let you come and visit me. You could come in the summer."

"No," he said. "We go to Walberswick."

"Where?"

He was pleased at remembering this, and thought it

strange that she shouldn't know. "We go to Walberswick," he repeated.

The afternoon nurse came in and began to gather up his toys. She put them in a cardboard box. "You must be washed now, to look nice for your aunt," she said, smiling at Oliver.

"I've had my bath." The nurse handed him his bath-robe and started to put slippers on his feet. He said, "I've *had* my bath," and when she persisted, grasping his foot, he kicked her with the foot that was free.

"How can you be so naughty when you're going home?" said the nurse. She turned to Mrs Chapman, aggrieved. "He has always been so good. I think we have spoiled him. Did you see what he did? *Un coup de pied!*"

"I should leave him alone if I were you," Mrs Chapman said.

Oliver had by now thrown bathrobe and slippers on the floor and retreated under the bedclothes.

"He's never been like this," the nurse kept saying, and Mrs Chapman kept answering, "I'm sure it hasn't been properly explained."

It seemed to Oliver high time that they stopped all this, and high time that his mother came to fetch him away. If Auntie Cath took him, his mother wouldn't know where he was. The taking away of the toys, the unscheduled attempt to wash him suggested that something unusual was about to take place. It could only mean his mother. When the door opened and he heard the voice of Auntie Cath, he stiffened and held the bedclothes, prepared to resist.

JEUX D'ETE

❖

❖

LATE in the afternoon, when their work was done, the young men of the town sailed their boats along the coast, out past the big hotels where foreigners stayed. They drifted in a wide, restless half circle around the private beaches belonging to the hotels. They liked to look at the foreign people and at the girls. The foreigners carried portable radios and smoked expensive cigarettes and their voices — French, German and English — floated over the calm Adriatic bays and rocky shore. The hotels, up on a low cliff behind the beaches, were square and imposing, built before the war and the People's Revolution. Now the hotels were said to belong to the people, and it was perhaps because of this ownership that the people hung about at a distance, staring in. There were Yugoslavs as well as strangers in the hotels — well-to-do civil engineers, and meritorious members of the police — but the young men were not interested in any of them. One would have said, indeed, that they failed to see them.

The chief magnet those last, hot days of July was a trio of girls on the beach of the Hotel Marina. All day, every day, the girls lay, stretched like offerings, on the warm rocks, under a sun that bleached their hair and turned their faces brown. They had neat hair and straight teeth, and they wore frilly skirted bathing suits that covered the tops of their rather fat legs.

"American women are said to have the finest legs in the world," one of the dining-room waiters remarked, as if he had been deceived. He hung over the railing of the dining terrace, watching the three motionless girls. From the pocket of his white jacket he fished out two butts he had saved from the breakfast ashtrays. He offered one to his companion, another waiter, who lit both, flipping the match down among the bathers.

"They aren't women," his companion said. "They are little girls."

"They think they are women."

Nancy and Patty and Linda were conscious of being observed. Even without opening their eyes, they could tell when men were looking. They always smiled at the waiters — the right sort of smile, friendly but distant — and they swam cautiously, tentatively, around the anchored boats and the blond young men from town. Nancy and Patty were sisters; Linda was a friend. The three were being clucked through Europe by a Miss Baxter, a professional chaperon, who, though careful, had decided that no harm could come to them on the beach, and had gone off to town today on the pretext of visiting churches. The girls had been looking at things in Italy and were shortly to be looking at things in Greece. They had looked at everything in Paris, in Nice, in Florence, in Rome and in Venice, all in less than four weeks. It had been cold in Paris and hot in Rome and smelly in Venice, and this beach, halfway down the Dalmatian coast, was the best part of the trip. They were good-tempered girls. They made no demands on the strange things they saw, or the strange people they met, and they had left a bland, favourable impression with the travel agents and consular officials with whom they had come in contact. To the undiscerning, they were alike as triplets. Miss Baxter could tell them apart, though. So could the boys in the boats.

Nancy and Patty lay with their eyes shut, silent, as if speech might interfere with the business of getting brown.

The advantages of having spent the summer abroad were easily outweighed by the fear that in the autumn they would be paler than their friends. Secretly, they wished they had stayed home and gone up to the lake; but it was a wish neither of them expressed, not even to each other. Someone had told them that there were no beaches in Greece — none, at least, where they would be staying. They were determined to grasp all the benefits possible from these few days of sun. Only Linda seemed unable to settle down. She looked at the sea and then up at the waiters. Suddenly she got up, with no explanation, and climbed the concrete steps that led up to the hotel. Her departure had the effect of a signal. The sisters behaved as if an inhibiting force had been removed. Patty rolled over, sighing. Nancy knelt, blinking. She looked at the shallow side of the rocks, and at the part where it was safe to dive.

"Going in?" said Patty.

Nancy shook herself like a little dog, cold at the thought of the water she would strike. She climbed to the top of the piled-up rocks, gathered courage and suddenly dived.

The boat nearest the beach was painted blue. One of the boys on board smoked a cigarette, the other sat with his feet over the side, moving them in the colourless water. He watched the girl who was swimming out to them. Both boys were fair, and nearly black with sun. Nancy caught a rope and, with the other hand, pushed back her dripping hair.

"I like your boat," she said.

"Come on, then," said the boy with the cigarette. He bent over and held out his hand.

"Uh-uh." She shook her head vigorously. Her eyelashes were stuck together in points with water. The boy with the cigarette lay prone. He edged closer to the side. He looked at her and then, suddenly giving up, lowered his head on his crossed arms.

"Come with us," said his friend, slowly, with great concentration. He had to fish each word from a sea teeming with English expressions.

"Oh, for goodness' sake," said the girl. "Can't a person even talk about your boat without starting something?"

The boy smoking had not understood. He said to his friend, "Ask her to come for a sail. Tell her we'll go around the island."

His friend shook his head impatiently, and the girl let go of the rope. She pushed herself out with a long backstroke and then turned over and swam to shore. They watched her pick her way out on the shallow side of the pier, over rocks perilous with sea urchins.

The boy smoking threw his cigarette into the calm water. He said, "Why does she always come out, then? They're crazy, I think."

"The other girl would come," said his friend. He looked at the dry rocks above the shore, where Linda, back from the hotel, was settling down on a towel. "That's the one," he said, with an assurance that would not have surprised the sisters. Men had followed the girls in Italy, but only Linda's door had been nearly broken down. She was not prettier, or fairer, or better dressed. But she was the one Miss Baxter watched, and, with a resigned concession to the workings of nature, so so did Nancy and Patty.

It took Linda, as always, about three minutes to arrange herself on a beach towel. "I've had a letter," she said, at last. "Remember that reporter we met in Florence, the one that was taking pictures for that Italian magazine?"

The sisters exchanged a look. The reporter, like every other man encountered on the trip, had shown an undisguised preference for Linda. "He wants to know if we're coming back through Italy," she went on. "They're trying out a new kind of submarine in Genoa or someplace. He wants me to go down in it, in the submarine. He says he'll take my picture. As he says, how can you make a submarine interesting all by itself? He says the story needs me. He says they'll put me on the cover."

"On what cover?" said Nancy. She longed to ask how he had known where to write, but felt it an unnecessary diversion.

"Oh, of some magazine."

The sisters were silent. They were by no means plain, and it seemed unfair that Linda should have everything. One of us would have had a chance if Linda hadn't been along, Nancy thought.

"I've cabled home," Linda said. "That's why I went up to the hotel just now. I thought I'd better do it and get it over with. I've asked my parents if it's all right. Baxie wasn't around, so I sent the cable myself."

"Why a cable?" said Patty. "Couldn't you have just written?"

"He wants an answer right away. Anyway, it's better to have your parents' consent; it's only polite. You sort of have to have it," said Linda, calmly, as if she were frequently involved in these emergencies. "I cabled, 'Offered chance to go down in new-type submarine for magazine cover please cable immediate permission.' Soon as I get the answer, I'll tell him yes."

"Well, I suppose your parents would hardly refuse," said Patty. "I mean, it's a once-in-a-lifetime chance."

"They might," said Linda, frowning. "They don't know it's a responsible sort of submarine, with officers and everything. They don't know there're going to be reporters and people around, and they don't know it isn't going to cost them any more money. I couldn't get all that in."

"You could have got in 'expenses paid,'" said Nancy.

"Anyway, they probably wouldn't mind if they did have to pay something, for a thing like that."

"I wouldn't ask them for more money," said Linda, virtuously.

At this point, a display of virtue was insupportable.

"*Naturally* you wouldn't ask for any more," said Nancy. "*Naturally*. It happens to be free." She added, "You didn't even tell them which navy it was."

"I forgot."

After a silence, Patty said. "I'll bet your parents won't want you to be on the cover. Ours certainly wouldn't."

"No," said Nancy, "and what's more I wouldn't like it. Not for myself."

"Neither would I," her sister said.

"Well, it wouldn't be either of you, anyway," said Linda, "so it doesn't matter." She lay flat on her back, looking dreamily — but with slightly narrowed eyes, as if there were calculation in the dream — up to the fringe of pine that hung over the edge of the cliff. There was so much truth in her remark that the others were not offended. Linda's success was inevitable, she would be famous first, married first, everything first. Unable to compete, they tacitly decided to share the excitement of her career.

"Wait till Baxie hears it," Patty said. "She'll be thrilled. It's a lot more exciting than her old churches."

"Poor Baxie," Linda said, closing her eyes, giving herself up to the deliciousness of sun and of being pretty and desired. "Churches are Baxie's kind of fun, I guess."

As it happened, Miss Baxter was spending the afternoon in a café. The café was on a square facing what seemed to be a very old church. Conscientiously, she noted every feature of the church and of the square, so that she could tell the girls about it later on. The girls were not allowed to sit in cafés. They had promised their parents before sailing. Cozy with guilt, Miss Baxter wondered if she was being fair in enjoying something her charges were not permitted. Returning to her exercise in observation, she recorded swallows, two sailors in uniform, a Gothic fountain, the absence of motorcars, and the fact that every window shutter on the square was painted the same shade of green. She was in a mood to find everything lovely; the glass she drank from seemed enchanting, and a poster announcing a summer festival with the words "SUMMER GAMES — JEUX D'ETE" struck her as being something of great significance and charm.

Her companion, a shabby gentleman from a tourist office, ordered slivovitz for them both. He was fat and amiable and anxious to improve his English. He carried a dictionary and looked everything up before he spoke. Miss Baxter gravely assisted him. To her charges, she appeared plain and effaced. However, the man from the tourist office was not the first to have asked for help with the English language. Miss Baxter's blue eyes held a kind of watery sympathy. She wore soft pastel suits with felt flowers pinned to the lapel, and blouses with pleated jabots. Part of the year, she taught history in a girls' boarding school. Summers, she hired herself out as a governess, chaperon, companion — anything that promised a season of travel or country living. This summer was particularly wonderful, for the girls' parents had let her choose the travel plan and given them all a large allowance. She was almost excruciatingly grateful. Three times a week she sent the parents a dull, detailed account of the places they had visited and the things they had seen. "We particularly enjoyed seeing the lovely Gold Staircase of Venice," she had written. "Linda was intrigued by the amusing round hats worn by the Italian gentlemen of the Renaissance. In the morning we hired a gondola.

The girls were amused at the bargaining required in hiring this conveyance. Nancy remarked..." Three times a week she put this sort of thing in the post, closing each letter with her fulsome thanks. She wanted to thank the parents, but she also wanted to let them know that they were getting their money's worth. When she was with the girls, she talked incessantly. She felt that she was not doing her duty or earning her keep if she kept a single impression to herself. Sometimes, talking on and on, she obliterated the scene she was so anxious they should take away with them. She had been deeply moved in Venice by a small thing, the reflection of water from the canal outside shining on the ceiling of the room. She had pointed it out to the girls, one of whom had said indulgently, "Honestly, Baxie!" Yet she remembered it now, and she remembered Florence because for breakfast she had been given a fresh fig that was cold as water and tasted of cream. She also remembered how the bootboy in Florence had pointed to her bed, then her, then himself, then clasped his hands and put his head against them.

"Did you care for Italy?" said her companion politely. He waved a fly away from his drink.

Miss Baxter considered her answer with care. The Croats and the Italians, she knew, were traditional enemies. "It is difficult to travel in a Latin country with a party of girls," she said. Her drink smelled of warm fruit. She drank the last of it and felt patches of heat covering her cheeks.

He smiled sympathetically and said, "It will be different here."

"I know." Tears started to her eyes. How kind he was, how kind they all were, how kind the Florentine bootboy had been, how lovely the swallows were, swooping across the square!

"We are not like the Italians," he said. The waiter took

away their small glasses and set fresh drinks before them.

"Thank goodness for that," Miss Baxter murmured, not really listening.

"Our boys are good boys," the man said. What he next had to say he assembled from his dictionary. Miss Baxter sipped her new drink, smiling at everyone. He had found the words: "I should say that, with our people, what matters is only the pure animal pleasure of making love." Uttered in bald English, it sounded quite wrong. Hastily, he ruffled his dictionary again.

"I'm sure," said Miss Baxter, still dreamy. The word "pure" had taken hold and she derived a sleepy pleasure from the idea of her girls purely in love. She had been so often in love herself, and fell so easily into romantic difficulties! The man from the tourist bureau seemed in no hurry to get back to work. Miss Baxter was perfectly content to sit on beside him. Conversation became at once halting and discursive: she remembered that they represented countries politically apart. Although not in the least politically minded, it seemed to her natural that the subject might arise, and destroy this new relationship — warm, sleepy, pleasantly sensuous. It was possible that he, too, felt this constraint. Their talk became slower. An awareness of what they were really about, and of what this was bound to lead to, surrounded them like — Miss Baxter thought — a warm little cloud. All the same, it made it difficult to get on with the normal interchange of polite speech, particularly between strangers who barely spoke the same tongue. It was almost seven o'clock before the lengthening shadows of buildings on the square reminded her of how long she had been away. Yawning, her companion paid for their drinks. For the moment, they were glad to part.

The man from the tourist office admired her frilled blouse. "Our women are like men," he said, holding her hand. "It is your femininity we find appealing." The "you" was collective — Miss Baxter was too modest to accept the entire tribute for herself — yet something like intimacy established itself, as if they had been though danger together, and Miss Baxter, brushing something invisible from her cheek, agreed that femininity was important. They made an appointment to meet on Sunday.

"It is our last day," she said, already savouring Sunday, and feeling warmly sad at the parting to follow.

Panic came during the walk back to the hotel. The road from town was long and hot, and the flaming oleanders cast a thin lacy shade. How could she have left her girls alone, on the beach, for an entire afternoon? I cannot be trusted, she thought. It was a thought she wore with comfort. It became her, like the curly lines of her clothes and the almost liquid anxiety in her eyes. She thought about Sunday, and the man from the tourist office. He was fat and affable. He was a *kind* man, she thought, halting in a patch of shade. But her charges, her girls! They might have drowned, or had indigestion, or disappeared in a sailboat with the blond young men from town. The pure animal pleasure of making love, the man had said. Perhaps he had been trying to warn her. The trouble had been his voice, so very reassuring, it had prevented her from taking in the import of his words. By the time she reached the hotel, anxiety was like a rope around her throat, and her voice, when she asked the desk clerk if he had seen her girls, was hoarse and uncontrolled.

"Your girls are here," said Linda, behind her. They had dressed for the evening in fresh, cool blouses and skirts. Their hair, streaked with sun and salt, was brushed, their lips rouged and expectant. Their expectancy terrified Miss Baxter; they seemed to her terribly in danger. I left them alone for most of a day in a country where anything might happen, she said to herself, but even as she produced the thought, she knew that the danger she had left them exposed to was not political. The truth was that she herself had always been expectant, still was (What about Sunday? What about the man from the tourist bureau?), and her life was strewn with errors and moves of unsurpassable stupidity.

"Oh, Baxie!" Nancy cried, falsely enthusiastic. "Guess what! Linda's been asked to go down in a submarine, and she's cabled home for permission."

Even if I were perfectly sober and could consider this rationally, Miss Baxter thought, I could not consider myself a greater failure than at this moment.

"I wish you had discussed it with me first," she said. "It was up to me to send the cable. What will Linda's parents think of me? After all they've spent."

"It's not going to cost them anything," Linda said sulkily.

"I mean, after all they've spent for me," said Miss Baxter. "Oh, I cannot bear it. No, no, don't tell me who has invited Linda to go down in a submarine. One of those boys in the sailboats..."

They denied it together, indignant. Linda said, "Honestly, Baxie, when you get like that, a person doesn't know what to do with you. It's not your fault. You couldn't help it if he asked me."

"Who?"

"This reporter," Nancy said. "You know, the one we met in Florence. The one that told us to be careful in Italy not to talk to married men."

"Yes, but then we met this other man, remember?" said her sister. "That sort of nice married man with the moustache, on the train, the one that told us never to talk to *single* men?"

Miss Baxter was not to be diverted. "I said nothing in any of my letters home about a reporter. What on earth are your parents going to think now? If only you girls would try to understand my position, my...my position," she said.

"Oh, Bax," said Linda, affectionately. She put her arm about Miss Baxter's shoulders and said, "What's your position, Baxie?"

The elating effect of the slivovitz had worn off just enough to give her a headache. But she still retained an alcoholic feeling of clarity. "My position is that I owe your parents a great deal in return for this trip. Your position is that you are spoiled, silly and rich."

She spoke so quietly that it was a moment or so before any of the girls realized a scene had been created. They looked at one another. They considered her reference to money indelicate in the extreme, but none of them could say so. They had been brought up to deprecate extravagance and to say that they couldn't afford things. Also, they felt that Baxie had no right to divert attention from Linda to herself. This was Linda's moment; even Baxie, unworldly though she was, ought to realize it.

In silence they filed out to the dining terrace for dinner. In silence they attempted to sulk; but they kept forgetting they were annoyed and even found themselves commenting on Miss Baxter's description of a church.

"How long will we be in Greece?" Linda said.

"A week."

"A whole week!" It was impossible to tell whether her exclamation meant joy or dismay.

"A whole week for all of Greece," Miss Baxter said. "Then back to Paris and home. We shall have had the best of it by then. August is so hot. We've had the best part of the summer. There's only tomorrow here and then Sunday, our last day."

"Our last day," Nancy said, working herself up to a feeling of nostalgia.

"I'll have my answer by then," Linda said, looking dreamily out to the warm summer sea. "I'll have my cable and I can tell him yes, and then we'll have Greece and then there's my submarine. Oh, Baxie!"

"I know," Miss Baxter said. "Only don't count on it, Linda dear."

But this was so preposterous that none of them bothered to reply.

WHEN WE WERE
NEARLY YOUNG

❖

❖

IN Madrid, nine years ago, we lived on the thought of money. Our friendships were nourished with talk of money we expected to have, and what we intended to do when it came. There were four of us — two men and two girls. The men, Pablo and Carlos, were cousins. Pilar was a relation of theirs. I was not Spanish and not a relation, and a friend almost by mistake. The thing we had in common was that we were all waiting for money.

Every day I went to the Central Post Office, and I made the rounds of the banks and the travel agencies, where letters and money could come. I was not certain how much it might be, or where it was going to arrive, but I saw it riding down a long arc like a rainbow. In those days I was always looking for signs. I saw signs in cigarette smoke, in the way ash fell and in the cards. I laid the cards out three times a week, on Monday, Wednesday and Friday. Tuesday, Thursday and Saturday were no good, because the cards were mute or evasive; and on Sundays they lied. I thought these signs — the ash, the smoke and so on — would tell me what direction my life was going to take and what might happen from now on. I had unbounded belief in free will, which most of the people I knew despised, but I was superstitious, too. I saw inside my eyelids at night the nine of clubs, which is an excellent card, and the ten of hearts, which is better, morally speaking, since it implies gain through effort. I saw the aces of clubs and diamonds, and the jack of diamonds, who is the postman. Although Pablo and Pilar and Carlos were not waiting for anything in particular — indeed, had nothing to wait for, except a fortune

61

—they were anxious about the postman, and relieved when he turned up. They never supposed that the postman would not arrive, or that his coming might have no significance.

Carlos and Pablo came from a town outside Madrid. They had no near relatives in the city, and they shared a room in a flat on Calle Hortaleza. I lived in a room along the hall; that was how we came to know each other. Pilar, who was twenty-two, the youngest of the four of us, lived in a small flat of her own. She had been married to Carlos's stepbrother at seventeen, and had been a widow three years. She was eager to marry again but feared she was already too old. Carlos was twenty-nine, the oldest. Pablo and I came in between.

Carlos worked in a bank. His salary was so small that he could barely subsist on it, and he was everywhere in debt. Pablo studied law at the University of Madrid. When he had nothing to do, he went with me on my rounds. These rounds took up most of the day, and had become important, for, after a time, the fact of waiting became more valid than the thing I was waiting for. I knew that I would feel let down when the waiting was over. I went to the post office, to three or four banks, to Cook's and American Express. At each place, I stood and waited in a queue. I have never seen so many queues, or so many patient people. I·also gave time and thought to selling my clothes. I sold them to the gypsies in the flea market. Once I got a dollar-fifty for a coat and a skirt, but it was stolen from my pocket when I stopped to buy a newspaper. I thought I had jostled the thief, and when I said "Sorry" he nodded his head and walked quickly away. He was a man of about thirty. I can still see his turned-up collar and the back of his head. When I put my hand in my pocket to pay for the paper, the money was gone. When I was not standing in queues or getting rid of clothes, I went to see Pilar. We sat out on her balcony when it was fine, and next to her kitchen stove when it was cold. We were not ashamed to go to the confectioner's across the street and bargain in fractions of pennies for fifty grams of chocolate, which we scrupulously shared. Pilar was idle, but restful. Pablo was idle, but heavy about it. He was the most heavily idle person I have ever known. He was also the only one of us who had any money. His father sent him money for his room and his meals, and he had an extra allowance from his godfather, who owned a hotel on one of the coasts. Pablo was dark, curly-haired and stocky, with the large head and opaque eyes you saw on the streets of Madrid. He was one of the New Spaniards — part of the first generation grown to maturity under Franco. He was the generation they were so proud of in the newspapers. But he must be — he *is* — well over thirty now, and no longer New. He had already calculated, with paper and pencil, what the future held, and decided it was worth only half a try.

We stood in endless queues together in banks, avoiding the bank where Carlos worked, because we were afraid of giggling and embarrassing him. We shelled peanuts and gossiped and held hands in the blank, amiable waiting state that had become the essence of life. When we had heard the ritual "No" everywhere, we went home.

Home was a dark, long flat filled with the sound of clocks and dripping faucets. It was a pension, of a sort, but secret. In order to escape paying taxes, the owners had never declared it to the police, and lived in perpetual dread. A girl had given me the address on a train, warning me to say nothing about it to anyone. There was one other foreign person — a crazy old Englishwoman. She never spoke a word to me and, I think, hated me on sight. But she did not like Spaniards any better; one could hear her saying so when she talked to herself. At first we were given meals, but after a time, because the proprietors were afraid about the licensing and the police, that stopped, and so we bought food and took it to Pilar's, or cooked in my room on an alcohol stove. We ate rationed bread with lumps of flour under the crust, and horrible ersatz jam. We were always vaguely hungry. Our craving for sweet things was limitless; we bought cardboard pastries that seemed exquisite because of the lingering sugary taste they left in the mouth. Sometimes we went to a restaurant we called "the ten-peseta place" because you could get a three-course meal with wine and bread for ten pesetas — about twenty-three cents then. There was also the twelve-peseta place, where the smell was less nauseating, although the food was nearly as rank. The décor in both restaurants was distinctly unEuropean. The cheaper the restaurant, the more cheaply Oriental it became. I remember being served calves' brains in an open skull.

One of the customers in the ten-peseta restaurant was a true madman, with claw hands, sparse hair and dying skin. He looked like a monkey, and behaved like one I had known, who would accept grapes and bananas with pleasure, and then, shrieking with hate at some shadowy insult, would dance and gibber and try to bite. This man would not eat from his plate. He was beyond even saying the plate was poisoned; that had been settled long ago. He shovelled his food onto the table, or onto pieces of bread, and scratched his head with his fork, turning and muttering with smiles and scowls. Everyone sat still when he had his seizures — not in horror, even less with compassion, but still, suspended. I remember a coarse-faced sergeant slowly lowering his knife and fork and parting his heavy lips as he stared; and I remember the blankness in the room — the waiting. What will happen next? What does it mean? The atmosphere was full of cold, secret marvelling. But nobody moved or spoke.

We often came away depressed, saying that it was cheaper and pleasanter to eat at home; but the stove was slow, and we were often too hungry to linger, watching water come to the boil. But food was cheap enough; once, by returning three empty Valdepeñas wine bottles, I bought enough food for three. We ate a lot of onions and potatoes — things like that. Pilar lived on sweet things. I have seen her cook macaroni and sprinkle sugar on it and eat it up. She was a pretty girl, with a pointed face and blue-black hair. But she was an untidy, a dusty sort of girl, and you felt that in a few years something might go wrong; she might get swollen ankles or grow a moustache.

Her flat had two rooms, one of which was rented to a young couple. The other room she divided with a curtain. Behind the curtain was the bed she had brought as part of her dowry for the marriage with Carlos's stepbrother. There was a picture of María Felix, the Mexican actress, on the wall. I would like to tell a story about Pilar, but nobody will believe it. It is how she thought, or pretended to think, that the Museo Romantico was her home. This was an extraordinary museum — a set of rooms furnished with all the trappings of the romantic period. Someone had planned it with love and care, but hardly any visitors came. If any did wander in when we were around, we stared them out. The cousins played the game with Pilar because they had no money and nothing better to do. I see Pilar sitting in an armchair, being elegant, and the boys standing or lounging against a mantelpiece; I say "boys" because I never thought of them as men. I am by the window, with my back turned. I disapprove, and it shows. I feel like a prig. I tip the painted blind, just to see the street and be reassured by a tram going by. It *is* the twentieth century. And Pilar cries, in unaffected anguish, "Oh, make her stop. She is spoiling everything."

I can hear myself saying grandly, "I don't want your silly fairy-tales. I'm trying to get rid of my own."

Carlos says, "I've known people like you before. You

think you can get rid of all the baggage — religion, politics, ideas, everything. Well, you won't."

The other two yawn, quite rightly. Carlos and I are bores.

Of them all, I understood Carlos best, but we quarrelled about anything. We could have quarrelled about a piece of string. He was pessimistic, and I detested this temperament; worse, I detested his face. He resembled a certain kind of Swiss or South African or New Zealander. He was suspicious and faintly Anglo-Saxon looking. It was not the English bun-face, or the Swiss canary, or the lizard, or the hawk; it was the unfinished, the undecided, face that accompanies the rotary sprinkler, the wet Martini, pussy-footing in love and friendship, expense-account foolery, the fear of the open heart. He made me think of a lawyer who had once told me, in all sincerity, "Bad things don't happen to nice people." It was certainly not Carlos's fault; I might have helped my prejudices, which I had dragged to Spain with my passport, but he could not help the way he looked. Pablo was stupid, but cheerful. Pilar was demented, but sweet. What was needed — we agreed to this many times — was a person who was a composite of all our best qualities, which we were not too modest to name. Home from the Romantic Museum, they made me turn out the cards. I did the Petit Jeu, the Square, the Fan, and the Thirteen, and the Fifteen. There was happy news for everyone except Carlos, but, as it was Sunday, none of it counted.

Were they typical Spaniards? I don't know what a typical Spaniard is. They didn't dance or play the guitar. Truth and death and pyromania did not lurk in their dark eyes; at least I never saw it. They were grindingly hard up. The difference between them and any three broke people anywhere else was in a certain passiveness, as though everything had been dealt in advance. Barring catastrophe, death and revolution, nothing could happen any more. When we walked together, their steps slowed in rhythm, as if they had all three been struck with the same reluctance to go on. But they did go on, laughing and chattering and saying what they would do when the money came.

We began keeping diaries at about the same time. I don't remember who started it. Carlos's was secret. Pilar asked how to spell words. Pablo told everything before he wrote it down. It was a strange occupation, considering the ages we were, but we hadn't enough to think about. Poverty is not a goad but a paralysis. I have never been back to Madrid. My memories are of squares and monuments, of things that are free or cheap. I see us huddled in coats, gloved and scarfed, fighting the icy wind, pushing along to the ten-peseta place. In another memory it is so hot that we can scarcely force ourselves to the park, where we will sit under elm trees and look at newspapers. Newspapers are the solace of the worried; one absorbs them without having to read. I sometimes went to the libraries — the British Institute and the American one — but I could not for the life of me have put my nose in a book. The very sight of poetry made me sick, and I could not make sense of a novel, or even remember the characters' names.

Oddly enough, we were not afraid. What was the worst that could happen? No one seemed to know. The only fear I remember was an anxiety we had caught from Carlos. He had rounded twenty-nine and saw down a corridor we had not yet reached. He made us so afraid of being thirty that even poor Pilar was alarmed, although she had eight years of grace. I was frightened of it, too. I was not by any means in first youth, and I could not say that the shape of my life was a mystery. But I felt I had done all I could with free will, and that circumstances, the imponderables, should now take a hand. I was giving them every opportunity. I was in a city where I knew not a soul, save the few I had come to know by chance. It was a city where the mentality, the sound of the language, the hopes and possibilities, even the appearance of the people in the streets, were as strange as anything I might have invented. My choice in coming here had been deliberate: I had a plan. My own character seemed to me ill-defined; I believed that this was unfortunate and unique. I thought that if I set myself against a background into which I could not possibly merge that some outline would present itself. But it hadn't succeeded, because I adapted too quickly. In no time at all, I had the speech and the movements and very expression on my face of seedy Madrid.

I was with Pablo more than anyone, but I remember Carlos best. I regret now how much we quarrelled. I think of the timorous, the symbolic, stalemate of our chess games. I was not clever enough to beat him, but he was not brave enough to win. The slowing down of our respective positions on the board led to immobility of thought. I sat nervously smoking, and Carlos sat with his head in his hands. Thought suspended, fear emerged. Carlos's terror that he would soon be thirty and that the affective part of his life had ended with so little to show haunted him and stunned his mind. He would never be anything but the person he was now. I remember the dim light, the racket in the street, the silence inside the flat, the ticking of the Roman-numbered clock in the hall. Time was like water dropping — Madrid time. And I would catch his fear, and I was afraid of the movement of time, at once too quick and too slow. After that came a revolt and impatience. In his company I felt something I had never felt before — actively northern. Seeing him passive, head on hands, I wanted to urge and exhort and beg him to do something: act, talk, sing, dance, finish the game of chess — anything at all. At no period was I as conscious of the movement and meaning of time;

and I had chosen the very city where time dropped, a drop from the roof of a cave, one drop at a time.

We came to a financial crisis at about the same moment. Pablo's godfather stopped sending money to him — that was a blow. Pilar's lodgers left. I had nothing more to sell. There was Carlos's little salary, but there were also his debts, and he could not be expected to help his friends. He looked more vaguely Anglo-Saxon, more unfinished and decent than ever. I wished there was something to kick over, something to fight. There was the Spanish situation, of course, and I had certainly given a lot of thought to it before coming to Spain, but now that I was here and down and out I scarcely noticed it. I would think, "*I am free,*" but what of it? I was also hungry. I dreamed of food. Pilar dreamed of things chasing her, and Pablo dreamed of me, and Carlos dreamed he was on top of a mountain preaching to multitudes, but I dreamed of baked ham and Madeira sauce. I suspected that my being here and in this situation was all folly, and that I had been trying to improve myself — my moral condition, that is. My financial condition spoke for itself. It was like Orwell, in Paris, revelling in his bedbugs. If that was so, then it was all very plain, and very Protestant, but I could not say more for it than that.

One day I laid out forty-eight cards — the Grand Jeu. The cards predicted treachery, ruin, illness, accidents, letters bringing bad news, disaster and pain.

I made my rounds. In one of the places, the money had come, and I was saved. I went out to the University, where the fighting had been, eleven or twelve years before. It looked like a raw suburban housing development, with its mud, its white buildings and puny trees. I waited in the café where Pablo took his bitter coffee, and when he came in I told him the news. We rode into the heart of Madrid on a swaying tram. Pablo was silent — I thought because he was delighted and overwhelmed; actually, he must have been digesting the astonishing fact that I had been expecting something and that my hanging around in banks was not a harmless mania, like Pilar in the Romantic Museum.

My conception of life (free will plus imponderables) seemed justified again. The imponderables were in my pocket, and free will began to roll. I decided, during the tram ride, to go to Mallorca, hire a villa, invite the three for a long holiday and buy a dog I had seen. We got down from the tram and bought white, tender, delicious, unrationed bread, weighed out by the pound; and three roasted chickens, plus a pound of sweet butter and two three-litre bottles of white Valdepeñas. We bought some nougat and chestnut paste. I forget the rest.

Toward the end of our dinner, and before the end of the wine, Carlos made one bitter remark: "The difference between you and us is that in the end something will always come for you. Nothing will ever come from anywhere for any of us. You must have known it all along."

No one likes to be accused of posturing. I was as irritated as I could be, and quickly turned the remark to his discredit. He was displaying self-pity. Self-pity was the core of his character. It was in the cards; all I could ever turn out for him were plaintive combinations of twos and threes — an abject fear of anonymous threats, and worry that his friends would betray him. This attack silenced him, but it showed that my character was in no way improved by my misfortunes. I defended myself against the charge of pretending. My existence had been poised on waiting, and I had always said I was waiting for something tangible. But they had thought I was waiting in their sense of the word — waiting for summer and then for winter, for Monday

70

and then for Tuesday, waiting, waiting for time to drop into the pool.

We did not talk about what we could do with money now. I was thinking about Mallorca. I knew that if I invited them they would never come. They were polite. They understood that my new fortune cast me out. There was no evasion, but they were nice about it. They had no plans, and simply closed their ranks. We talked of a longer future, remembering Carlos and his fear. We talked of our thirties as if we were sliding toward an icy subterranean water; as if we were to be submerged and frozen just as we were: first Carlos, then Pablo and me, finally little Pilar. She had eight years to wait, but eight would be seven, and seven six, and she knew it.

I don't know what became of them, or what they were like when their thirtieth year came. I left Madrid. I wrote, for a time, but they never answered. Eventually they were caught, for me, not by time but by the freezing of memory. And when I looked in the diary I had kept during that period, all I could find was descriptions of the weather.

BETTER TIMES

❖

❖

TURNING the old house over to Guy and Susan Osborne, Susan's Aunt Val said, "Children, have I mentioned this before? You may hear someone prowling in the garden at night. The place is stiff with smugglers now. They come down from Italy, along the top of that cliff." She pointed in the direction of the frontier — a handsome red cliff over which falcons cried and flew. Their shadows slid impartially on the fields of Italy and France. But Guy and Susan could not see anything except the dining-room wall. Along this wall, an army of red ants bore the foundations of the house up to the roof.

One day the house would fall, the walls tunnelled to paper. If it collapsed down on their heads at this moment, at lunch, Aunt Val would not have been surprised. Every crumb of wood, every floating speck of dust was disastrous. Aunt Val knew. Her hands flew out to the newly married pair in gestures of warning. Her hair was made of old doll stuffing; her hair net was down to her eyes. She was in true terror, not over the smugglers, or the ants, but lest Guy should demand the last of the macaroni-and-cheese. Guy could not know, of course, how important it was that the last of every dish be spooned onto one special, thick-rimmed china plate, and how this plate must be kept in the larder, in the dark, until the food upon it spoiled.

Hoping to distract him, glancing elsewhere, Aunt Val said, "Not only smugglers but, you know, Guy, *shiftless* young men. Young men without jobs, with nothing to do." That was tactless; Guy was also unemployed. "Italians, I mean to say," said Aunt Val hurriedly. "*They* wouldn't do a day's work if you offered solid gold." Would Guy? "I mean the sort of young men who would murder one for a pair of shoes!" the old lady cried. Whatever else you could say about poor dear Guy, he was no murderer.

So that was the autumn prospect. But Guy kept smiling, saying "Yes" and "Quite," turning his water glass around and around, as though being murdered for his shoes were part of the season's plan. Old Val could have been just a little more lavish, he thought. Water to drink, and the mucilage cheese. The house was full of ants, and the windows, which were dirty, were smeared with rain. The most disobliging sight in nature was provided by the view — palm trees under a dark sluice of rain. Beyond a drenched hedge stood a house exactly like Aunt Val's, with spires, minarets, stained-glass windows; possibly it, too, contained a drawing room stuffed with ferns and sheeted sofas. The houses were part of a genteel settlement, built in an era of jaunty Islamic-English design, in a back pocket of the Riviera country. The district was out of fashion, crumbling, but the houses persisted; dragging their rock gardens, their humped tennis courts, they marched down the slope of a tamed minor Alp.

In the old days, Aunt Val said, except for the trees and the climate and the conversation of servants, one needn't have ever known this was France. That was how they had liked being abroad then. "Abroad" meant keeping warm, pudding at Christmas, a mutable, merchants' England everywhere you went. The people in Villa Omar and Villa Khartoum had been rich but not received; they hadn't cared. They received one another for tennis parties and fat, starchy teas. Well, it was over, Aunt Val said. Now one knew this was France. There were enormous taxes to pay. Servants were scarce....

The conversation might have been in England. Yet it

was really France; thirty miles away was the true Riviera
— white houses bristling with balconies, yachts, flags. Guy
thought of that and pulled himself straighter in his chair.
Pale-eyed, old war hero, nearly successful salesman— of
nearly anything— he thought of the flags and the yachts,
and of the present, with its gains and rewards.

Susan was looking at the ants on the wall as if she were
in a dream. She fell naturally into pretty positions, although
she was not a truly pretty girl. In an ugly mood— which
Guy had still to see— she might resemble a pug; when her
face was not reflecting solemnity or inquisitiveness, it
tended to crumple. Her ideas, her affections, were based on
her having been all her life somebody's favourite god-
child or niece. Watchfulness made her seem without
expression. That look— empty, receptive— and her light,
straight hair caused her to be compared to a medieval
pageboy or a picture-book Anglo-Saxon girl, uncoarsened
by Norman blood. Even Guy, who was twenty-two years
older than his wife and surely centuries wiser, could
mumble about porcelain cheeks and silken hair. It exasperated her; she knew about reality— her father had
swindled a large sum of money once, and they had left
Kenya and never gone back. She had been told only that
they could never live out in Africa again, and that there
had been a plot, of which her father was the victim. No
one would help or trust him, or give him a job. Then both
parents died; more mystery. She persistently went back to
sources now, looking for specific explanations of so many
puzzling affairs. She was eighteen, and she had thought
that marriage was in itself an explicit sort of answer.

Guy was sure that Susan was not listening to Aunt Val.
He felt as if he had been left stranded at a party with the
only bore. He tried to touch her foot under the table. He
deplored Susan's constant worry and thought. As he said,
it put him off. It was all too deep. If only the poor little

thing had been through something really big—the war.

Susan looked at the ants, but she *was* listening to Aunt Val. Sometimes out of her aunt's dotty wanderings came one sharp, disconcerting observation—just what Susan liked. Here where there were palm trees under rain and cypresses as soaked as sponges there had once been a wilderness, with wild apricot and almond trees, and the olive groves left behind by the Greeks, Aunt Val said, and you could always tell where there had been a nice English garden by two things—cypress trees and palms. Now the gardens were going back to wilderness again. The suburban mountainside belonged to falcons, peasants, smugglers and a few survivors of the old days. But it was an ordered wilderness, properly reforested, with drains, and pampas grass, and *tout confort*.

Fortunately for Guy, who would not knowingly have entered any kind of wilderness, there would be people about, agreeable people, English-speaking—English, in fact. A neighbour, Major Terry, had been in to see them before lunch. Yellow-toothed, smelling of unwashed woollen garments and cold tobacco pipes, dragged by a slavering boxer dog on a lead, Major Terry entered the drawing room, sat on a sheeted sofa, and could not take his eyes away from Guy's wife. Susan had dropped, sulking, into her chair. She wore tight Italian trousers, a black pullover, beads. The costume was a reaction from the things she had been made to wear in school, and her slight, sullen commonness was a stand in favour of reality. "Be sure to bring your little *mem-sahib*," said the Major, inviting Guy to look at anything—a chicken run, a blue hibiscus, some bound issues of *Country Life*. There hadn't been anything like Susan about for years.

"Did you hear that man?" said Susan gravely, twisting the beads, after the Major had departed. "Did you hear what he called me? *'Mem-sahib,'* he said. Why it's a dream world, Guy, a horrid Shangri-La. *Mem-sahib!* Don't they *know?"*

Guy was unwise enough to say, "They don't. That's their charm." It was unwise because he risked appearing unredeemably old to his bride. He wished again that Susan would dream more and think less. Guy admired anyone's dream, whether it was the private dream that led to Monte Carlo and a yacht or the dream of Major Terry, who said *"mem-sahib"* and inhabited empires. But Susan, unequipped for dreams, congealed life for Guy by seeing things as they were. Perhaps she was too soon out of the schoolroom. Perhaps her clear stare was not medieval, after all, but just the righteous, prying look of the form prefect. He remembered how soon after their wedding she had begun to get the drift of things, particularly of his financial affairs. She had pushed a straight lock away from her face, kept her hand there, and said maternally, "Tell me, Guy. Are you *improvident?"*

Now they were here, down at Aunt Val's, because he was improvident and could not have kept a canary with style. They were in trouble and had no money for the rent in London—although Guy kept pretending it was all frolic and spree. They were to spend the autumn caretaking for Aunt Val while she, bewildered, went to stay with terrible cousins in Wales. The plan was Susan's; for such a baby, she had a good head. It happened that because of unfair competition from the Japanese, Guy's firm had retrenched, and he was out of a job. Now he was waiting. He was waiting for a rearrangement of the planets concerned with his fate, for his close-fisted mother to increase his allowance, and for better times. He was also waiting for a letter about a post with a British firm in the Argentine. (Oil-burners—odourless oil-burners. Guy said it was just up his street. Given a chance, he would be first-rate at selling odourless oil-burners in the Argentine.)

Out of habit, he pressed a nerve in his left hip, which had been injured in an air crash during the war. This pressure caused him sharp immediate pain but relieved a feeling of weight on his left knee. It was a trick he had learned. When he stood up to walk, his limp would be less pronounced.

"There is the gin," Aunt Val said suddenly. "It is of very poor quality, and I can't think how it came into the house. You will find it under the kitchen stairs. There must be thirty bottles still."

"Thirty bottles of gin?" said Guy.

"Under the stairs. But of poor quality. I am so sorry. Everything I am leaving you is poor." She apologized for the gin, for the smugglers, even the noise of the sea. The sea was miles behind them, but the cliff was a sounding board. Often, she promised them, and was sorry about it, they would hear the beating of phantom waves.

The smugglers' passage was a kind of game. Guy liked the sound of it. First there were the border police, and the guns, and then the steep clandestine path. The path forked, Aunt Val said. One branch led the fugitives to safety, by way of a burned olive grove, remnant of an old forest fire, and a peasant's house and then her house. The other branch, which seemed to be leading to the warm lights of a town, suddenly narrowed and merged with the wall of the cliff. Often a secret traveller missed his footing in the dark and was found killed on the rocks, with a sprig of broom in his hand, grasped in the fall. But Guy said it was fair enough; there was the same sporting chance one would allow an otter, a fox or a prisoner of war.

"Oh, stop it, Aunt Val," said Susan, not quite daring to bully Guy. "There haven't been any real smugglers around here for years. There isn't anything *to* smuggle, except drugs, and that's done in a big way now, in planes,

and boats. These smugglers are just wretched men from
Italy looking for work in France. The Italians won't let
them out and the French won't let them in, and so they
come as they can. They aren't dangerous. They are just
— *dispossessed*." She loved those words: improvident,
dispossessed.

Aunt Val looked at Guy. "Let us not lose our heads over
these people," her small, daft eyes implored. Guy would
have backed her all the way. Whatever he thought of
Aunt Val's luncheon, or whatever her opinion of him as a
provider for Susan, he and Aunt Val were the same kind.
They bore a dozen labels that said so. Silence, camou-
flage, self-control, a cruel tact — these were virtues they
had handled and that had tarnished in their hands. But
Susan would not admit these tarnished objects as virtues.
She confused her elders, set them running in moral
circles, like ants whose path has been interfered with.
They were too taken aback ever to say to her "How do you
know?" She denounced their judgments and prodded
their failings. Alas, they did not believe they had failed.
"As for Major Terry," she said suddenly, as if he were the
principal source of their going mentally soft and astray, "*I*
shall have nothing to do with him. He can stare all he
likes. If that drooling boxer could talk, it would have
more sense."

Aunt Val began to twitter about neighbourly kindli-
ness and borrowed gardening tools. Major Terry was kind
about sharing his television. Guy merely said, "Oh, I
don't know," preparing the defence of his autumn social
life. An invitation to the least promising party would
have sent him whistling into a clean shirt. People liked
him on sight, and there were always the drinks. He could
have slipped easily into life down here, or into any other.
He wondered if Susan knew.

"But you must be friendly, Susan, dear," said Aunt Val,

clasping the macaroni-and-cheese — saved — in her arms. "Everyone will love you. As for Guy, why, I can't count the friends he will make. Guy is so awfully nice."

Susan was about to explain that he wasn't so awfully nice, that she thought it was just the way he behaved. But she checked herself and held still. Curious, prodding, she was still not sure just how much grown people could stand being hurt.

Aunt Val went to Wales, bearing an empty bird cage she had promised the cousins years before, and two of the thirty bottles of inferior gin, so as to have refreshment during the voyage. Guy and Susan were left alone. They had not been married long, and there had been people around them in London. They went up and down stairs hand in hand, and Susan told him a little about her family — not too much. She was not certain what she ought to think. She told him what she suspected about life, and she unfolded her touchingly empty past. Guy told her about the war and, one evening, about a woman named Marigold. He had had a lot to drink, and one topic led to the next with sliding facility. Susan listened politely. She already knew. She had found a letter. Found? She systematically went through his pockets. After all, that was how schoolgirls learned to know each other well. Locked in a bathroom, she had read the letter and marvelled at the ability of a man to lead two lives, or two facets of the same life, without going off his head. She read that Marigold was drowning in her marriage but that the memory of Guy kept her afloat. For some reason that Susan did not understand, Guy and Marigold had not married each other. A landscape of middle-aged resignation came into view. She observed it with a cold eye. She was not jealous. Marigold was drowning, and Guy was hers.

Aunt Val sent instructions from Wales, mostly of an

economical, electricity-saving kind; the autumn rain continued to blow down from the Alps; and one day they were
nearly out of funds. Susan said, "Guy, about the letter. I
mean the letter about the job in the Argentine. You are
expecting it, aren't you? It *is* real?"

"Oh, real as real," he said affectionately — or perhaps
his tone was on the fringe of affection. It was terrible for
old hero Guy, so shady, slippery and gay — it was terrible
having a witness.

Luckily, there were the nights. At night he could still
promise anything she wanted and make her believe in the
prospect. He could give assurance of miracles. He promised that the next day would be better; the rain would
stop, the letter would come. As with most cheerful men,
his weak point was memory. He forgot at night what the
morning had been. Mornings, far from being better, as Guy
had said they would be, were the low point of their lives.
Everything he touched was icy or congealed. The coffee
grinder in his hands froze the blood. He held his fingers
over the gas ring where he made toast. It was hours before
he could bring himself to shave, because of the cold taps.
Susan stayed in bed with her cooling hot-water bottles. She
could make passable Turkish delight, but that wasn't called
for now. Aunt Val had left them a quantity of kumquat
jam, bottled — or at any rate labelled — by herself. Susan
observed with uncritical interest that Guy was expert in
not pushing credit too far. Occasionally he gave the grocer
a rest and they lived on toast and the gin and the kumquat
jam. He never minded. Susan had never seen him cast
down. Her father — the Kenya absconder — became small
and dark beside this sunny husband. Guy never protested
against injustice — that he was forty and had been thrown
out of his job, that he had a bad leg from the war and
would limp all his life. But no one can exist only as a
happy former hero. His real feelings were layers deep.

Under his manner was a pool of gall, unadmitted, opaque. Something had gone wrong for him just after the war, either in love, or ambition, or the way the world seemed when he got up from his bed and his plaster casts. Now he would never say he missed or wanted anything. His desire for Susan was a single exception, and, as there had been no one to forbid or advise her, she had been easily won. He liked every circumstance as it came along. If liking was impossible, then he blamed the weather — something beyond one's control. It was all the weather down here. Who would have believed the south of France could be chill and wet? If the weather would change, he and Susan might enjoy strolling down to the shops; otherwise, one could make a jolly meal of jam and toast. After a time, when the nights and the prospects inevitably failed, he said that if their beds were not so damp and Susan not so entrenched in hot-water bottles, love would not be in abeyance. It had nothing to do with Susan or him; it was all in the time of year.

They waited for the letter. Every night Susan heard the smugglers in the garden. She heard whispers, footsteps, and forgot that they were only the footsteps of the dispossessed. The certainty that she was being watched by strangers froze and held every scattered alarm, every inconsequential fear that in other circumstances would have briefly brushed by. She knew that to Guy her fears were puzzling and rather dowdy. They spoiled for him the red-and-ochre cliff over which smugglers came and falcons flew. She was afraid of strangers; it was virginal, queer. He could not understand. To him, unknown people were ghosts. He could feel neither pity nor fear where they were concerned; they did not expect it. Ghosts have no true feelings; they are mystifying, unreasonable, with no regard for privacy. The whispers in the dark, the footprints on the wet drive, the odd, abandoned clues — one shoe, or a filthy coat — were trappings of chaos. Ghosts and confusion. He was for order, and gaiety, and for dealing with living things.

For Susan's sake, he went around the garden every night with a light in his hand. Often he was bold and drunk, and if he had come face to face with a man — walked into a man and not a ghost — he would have clapped him on the shoulder, with the hearty air left over from the war, and given him a cigarette and plenty of good advice. He shone his light into the black roots of wisteria, frightening the rats, and on the palms. Sometimes there might have been a blur — a face — by the cypress windscreen, but he was so sure the night contained no threat to him that he never called out, but turned away and limped back along the drive. Under the caked wet leaves at his feet he could hear the stirrings of small things keeping out of the rain — black beetles, spiders. "Lizards," craven Susan would have said, confusing them with scorpions, probably — something that could kill with a sting. No use telling her the lizards were sleeping through the winter (rather like Guy and Susan that year) and that there were no scorpions in this part of France; none to speak of.

Susan cowered indoors, dressed for charades. She dressed as though she had simply forgotten what normal people put on their backs. One night, after seven weeks of waiting for the letter — a whole lifetime — Guy came into the house, unwinding his scarf, and called down the dark hall, "I've told you, there's nobody. Now be a good girl and give me some peace."

In the drawing room, lit like a pleasure boat, Susan knelt by the fire. She gave him a large-pupilled tipsy stare. Out of the fur fringe of an anorak hood, found in a trunk or a cupboard of Aunt Val's, her fine, straight hair sprang as if electrified. She had fastened a plaid blanket around her shoulders with a safety pin and a cameo brooch, but the brooch was open and dangling. She was down on the dove-grey rug she had stained with tea and burned with cigarettes trying to make toast on a long-handled, trembling fork. Everything he was capable of feeling about her, all the tenderness and the subdued exasperation, was called up by the sight of her now. She had been an enchanting girl, a medieval page. He had snatched her straight out of the schoolroom — quite a feat for a lame old boy. He had never wanted to marry anybody, but he could not have had her any other way. Marriage had seemed a small thing then — a sand flea. But Marigold had been right; his life was too dodgy for wives, and it was better without witnesses, alone.

Still, they were quite the picture of domestic heaven, he thought a moment later: Guy with his legs stretched toward the fire, a glass of gin in one hand and frightened Susan at his feet. Being tall, his usual view of people began with the top of the head. Susan's head — the porcelain skull, the true silk hair — had attracted him to her in the first place. He gently pushed her anorak hood away. His sentiments expanded with drink. He would have murmured some endearment, but she might turn the clear, unfocussed stare in his direction and say, "The letter, Guy. Are you really expecting it? Do you think it will come?"

Without looking up at him, attending to their toast, she said, "You know, Guy, I like being married and all that, but I think I would rather go back to London, if you don't mind. I like being married and everything, but I think I'm too young. I mean, I think I'd rather not be married any more." Often, alone, when Guy was asleep or looking at the television over at Major Terry's, she had wandered around the rooms and come across hibernating geckos — small house lizards — their heartbeats slowed until they were just this side of life. She turned them over, ungently, with the cruel curiosity of a child. Looking at them, she would think, Now, let me see, what am I doing? I am married to Guy Osborne and we are having a honeymoon in the south of France. Cruel, frightened, she looked up now to see what he would do.

He simply thought it was a good thing that she had decided to start a row at this moment, because he could hear someone walking in the drive and knew he would not be able to persuade her that it was the sound of a blown leaf. It was his habit to see the best in every circumstance — marriage being otherwise untenable.

He did not take her seriously. Being in the darkened winter south had led to too much brooding and talk. Every tree and stone seemed to be waiting, like them, for a minor change. But trees and stones have this advantage: they do not converse. There is talk and talk. Guy would have gone on about the war, which he had enjoyed, but Susan had got in first with her family, and her fears, and even Marigold. Poor Marigold, whom he had loved, now stuck like persistent bad luck to their marriage, their future, their uncertain life.

"Then, you see, you could just marry Marigold, and I could get a job in a coffee bar," said Susan, buttering toast.

"I couldn't and you certainly couldn't," he said. "I couldn't marry Marigold, even if I wanted to. Although the fact of the matter is, I adored her."

"You never got over her," Susan said. She had been saying this all along.

"In a way not. You see, we knew each other awfully well."

The prefect took over. "Then it would have been more honourable not to have married me. You needn't have. I wasn't *seduced*."

Guy seemed to accept this. He might have got over

Marigold in time, but never the war. Tonight's drinking and arguing brought it back. His closest friends had been killed, but he thought of them as living and young. He looked, and would always look, as if he were bringing in an aircraft with all the essential parts shot away. His war record was good for jobs, although for one reason or another, not Guy's doing, they never held up; and his manner still brought down women: flower women who sobbed in bars, forgot their own names, lost their purses; soft little women, appealing as tiny animals, usually married to hopeless men. The beloved Marigold, combining essentials, was both flower and mouse. Guy's ability to recall, exclusively limited to scenes of war, made way for memories of his love. In stormier, happier times, she edged from the bar counter to the telephone and returned in tears: the husband, at home and waiting for his dinner, had been cross. But Marigold, frail thing, was not to be shoved. She dried her tears and said she would have another drink. Guy admired that.

His wife had nothing of that fierce mouselike courage. She talked about leaving him, unsettled by gin probably, but wait!

"*You* should go, actually," said Susan, now in the ugly mood he thought of as exclusively possible with women. "It is *my* aunt's house." She thought of the letters Marigold had written to him that she had read in the freezing bathroom, perched uncomfortably on the edge of the tub. "I think you should go within twenty-four hours."

He paid no attention. She would not have stayed alone a second, and it would have taken him twenty-four days to decide where to go. He slipped the bottle, the last of their hostess's gin, behind his chair. He took a drink, shuddering. "Somebody's walked on my grave," he said amiably. Obviously he never expected to have a grave, anywhere. Susan seemed to him terribly comic, telling him to clear out that way, with the plaid blanket rakishly tossed back. He could not help giving her a friendly smile.

The smile was maddening. He reacted no more than a sleeping lizard that, tormented, could not move an eye or a frozen limb. Unable to adjust his eyes to a fixed point, Guy placidly watched a transparent Susan detach herself from his wife and slip to one side. Interested, but not alarmed, his reflexes all one minute behind, he saw Susan and her double smash a clock. They could never replace that clock.

The awaited collapse came on. Susan sobbed on his lap.

"Poor little kitten!"

"You never got over Marigold. You should never have married me."

"Oh, come on. You can love different people different ways."

"I didn't think being married to you would be like this."

"Neither did I," said Guy, truthfully. "Don't cry, now. You get so worked up at night. Everything will be different in the morning."

But she shook her head—no. The weight of their marriage shifted; she rejected the promises and remembered the claims. They were sliding, as a couple, from being the gay relations from London, caretaking for a lark, to the improvident kin who must be helped; they were slipping over an invisible frontier. On one side were people with funny little debts (as Guy pretended he and Susan were) and on the other were the people who wanted such a lot but weren't able to pay for any of it.

She said helplessly, "It's just that I think I'm too young."

"Too young to be alone in London, if that's what you mean."

He remembered how she had daunted her elders, how moral she had been. Patiently he explained their present situation all over again. He had lost his job because of competition from the Danes—no, the Japanese; the Danes last time—and they had thought it would be fun to wait for better times in the South. They had given up their flat in London—remember? Susan remembered. Of course Guy was right....He was endlessly tender and kind. He must have been like that in the old days when he was prying Marigold out of bars. *Guy* was the one with the grasp on fact.

She decided to blame the house. It was far too big. One of them was always wondering what the other one was up to. If one had nothing to do and found the other occupied, the unoccupied person felt abandoned. Drawn to the warmth of the single fire, they met in the drawing room at half past five. To avoid running up a reproachable electrical bill, they kept all but the drawing room dark, giving the rest of the house over to the wind, and the scratching sounds. The area around the fireplace was cleared, the uncovered tables crowded with full ashtrays. The rest of the furniture was still hidden under sheets. On dim corner tables, jars of drooping, blackish carnations were the reminders of Susan's early efforts to make the room alive.

"All the same," she said, snivelling, drying her tears with the palms of her hands, "I know you think about Marigold. Sometimes I believe you would murder me to get rid of me, if you dared." He did not reply. He looked suddenly old and ill. It was no good; nobody was planning to murder anybody. Guy had a bad leg and hip. The cold was worse for him than for Susan, although he never mentioned it. He was waiting for news from the world;

for a message. Submerged in the icy lake of his situation, he accepted this stunning shock: he was forty, he had never been able to earn a living, and in a moment of sexual insanity he had taken on a young, young wife.

As Guy had promised all along, the weather cleared in the night. A mistral blew in from the sea, sending the clouds inland to pile up against the higher Alps. It was dryly cold. Susan stood out on the terrace before the drawing room and saw that torn, stained newspapers were flapping against the hedge. Someone had been through in the night. The wind dragged at her hair. She felt everything swept back and away; her marriage was knocked down and the threadroots picked up by the wind. In the drawing room was the wreckage of the short quarrel — the smashed clock.

Evidently miracles occurred. There was a letter, and it was not from Aunt Val. She watched Guy's progress up the drive from the road, where he had been waiting for the postman to come by, as he did every day. He came up to the terrace and stood with his arm around Susan. The letter fluttered against her arm. Susan would not read it; she would take his word.

They began walking up and down the terrace arm in arm. The letter was from Guy's mother; she was sending them money, and they were to join her for the winter in Madeira. His mother was taking over from Susan's relatives; an implicit, unspoken volley was beginning. He told Susan that his mother was mean; she had always kept him on short rein, and his father before him. It was puzzling, hearing him talk about allowances as if he were a little boy. For if the house had fallen, or if Susan's hair had caught fire, he would surely have known what to do. It was just this business of earning a living, keeping jobs. They talked about Madeira, confusing it with the future in the Argentine. Susan believed. He had said the letter would come; it came. He had said the weather would change. She did not know of any more reliable prophets, or even if any existed. They agreed that everything would be different once they had made a move. They would be careful about the house they lived in — not too large, not too old; it made all the difference. Where they were going now, Guy was saying, there would be no difficulty about the climate; they would never have the weather between them again. Guy had been told it was sunny all the year around.

A Question
Of Disposal

❖

❖

BELIEVING that she was dying, and certain she would die before the end of the year, Mrs Glover told her son Digby to choose the place they — she and Digby and Janet, his fiancée — would go to for their holiday in June. Digby's and Janet's vacation problems were beyond her now; they would have to begin making plans of their own.

But all the decisions of Digby's life, save one, had been made by his mother. Greatly dismayed by the prospect of freedom, the cause of which he had not been informed, he carried a number of Royal Automobile Club maps into his mother's sitting room and spread them on the floor. Crouching, he stared at the black tracings — the winding highways, the names of strange towns. Here there would be mountains, he said to himself, and that was certainly the sea. It seemed to him that he and his mother and Janet had been to every possible country, and had started over from the beginning years before. His hands, shuffling the maps, were aimless and weather-burned; his shrug had something of the adolescent's "Leave me alone." Digby was thirty-four.

"There," he said, having made, he thought, a picture of Western Europe, with most of the pieces in place. He looked up, smiling, with one hand over Spain. He held a cigarette in the other hand, and tried to be careful about the ash; but he was not careful enough, and his mother watched without saying anything as it lengthened and fell.

Because Mrs Glover never quite asked for anything she

wanted, or said plainly what she would like, Digby could not know now that she did not wish to go abroad at all. If this was to be her last June, as the doctors had said it might be, she wanted to spend it in London, listing the furniture and the linen and preparing instructions about the change from summer to winter curtains. He felt the weight of an unexplained silence, and supposed that even though he had said nothing except "There," it had probably been the wrong thing. He returned his attention to the floor and its terrible possibilities. He could not understand these maps, which were so simple when he was driving somewhere and had been told where to go, and so muddy when they presented a conundrum, as they did today. He rocked on his toes, whistled, shifted his hand, saw where it had been resting. He said he expected they could go to Spain.

"You and Janet met in Spain," said Mrs Glover. "Is that why you want to go back there now?"

Digby had forgotten about having ever met her any-where. He did not say so. He could not always tell where his mother was leading him, and had learned to take care.

"Oh, Janet," he said; or it may have been "*Old* Janet." The tone suggested the second.

Looking down on Digby, Mrs Glover remembered her death, with the satisfaction of someone whose mouth is obstinately closed on a secret. She knew that everyone, including old Janet, would be shocked and astonished when they heard of her long, concealed decline. She knew they would say that her death was a blessing for Digby and a release. Without his mother to thwart him, Digby would do whatever he liked. But Digby did not want to do anything. Crouched at his mother's feet, he seemed to her as incapable of deciding anything as the day he was born. Murmuring over his maps, burning holes in the carpet, he represented not so much a piece of her heart as one of her last commissions on earth. Mrs Glover had lived for many years as though expecting to be run over by a bus; her affairs were in order. She believed she could have died in a minute, without a word of complaint, had there not remained two questions of disposal. One was this house in London, which she cherished; the other was Digby, her bachelor son.

The disposal of Digby caused her anxiety, but the fate of the house caused her pain. Digby, though puzzled, would not mourn her long. He would continue driving about in hairy pullovers and gym shoes, and reading publications about motoring, and he would go on contributing to one of them — mostly paragraphs about restaurants in which he had luckily not been swindled. He would say that his mother had gone to a better place, and that he was bound to turn up there, too, eventually. That was the total Digby, in his mother's eyes, except for one unexplained action. One night, seven years ago, in a village in Spain, Digby had become engaged to healthy Janet Crawley, who, with three other girls from her office, was staying at the Glovers' hotel. For a time, Mrs Glover had feared he might actually marry Janet. She had no great fear of losing Digby but did not want to acquire Janet as well. She had feared he might marry Janet; now that she knew she was dying, she feared he never would.

Digby must marry Janet for the sake of the house. It was a narrow, three-storied house, to which she had given all the obsessive passion she had once felt for India. A perfectionist, she could not really love a human being. Human beings were imperfect, and resisted her. Something in the nature of people — even Digby's nature — said "Hands off." India had been a vast idea, and Indians dying were poetic; but then they tried to trade mystery for politics, and lost Mrs Glover. But the house was herself. It had not opposed her, and was unlikely to disappoint her or develop a will of its own. She had it on a ninety-five-year leasehold, which was certainly longer than one could ever expect to keep a husband or a son. The lease would not expire until 2032; Digby would fill at least thirty years of the span — forty, if Janet looked after him — and then, unless poor Janet had waited too long to marry, there would be heirs. Until 2032, then, the house must stand. Mrs Glover's shade would be there, but she could not depend on its powers. Her husband had died, her friends had vanished; she doubted the powers of ghosts.

Digby, still breathing heavily and talking to himself, traced the eastern coast of Spain with his thumb. "We could go where we went that other time," he said, pursuing his bright idea. "Where I met Janet, as you say."

"Did you like Spain?"

"You don't have to like a place just because you go there for holidays," he said.

"Tell me something else then. Think before you answer. Do you like this room?"

Digby looked around him and said, "It's not bad, but all that pale stuff gets dirty."

"What about Janet? Has Janet ever said anything about the room?"

"*I* don't know. She asked me if all the stuff was ours, once. I mean from our people. I told her no, from antique places and auctions. I told her it was something like Georgian and French. I suppose that was right."

"Would Janet mind about its being so pale if she lived here?"

"Janet probably has things fixed the way she wants them at home," he said reasonably. "Tell me if it's all right about Spain. I've got to fix it up with old Janet and fix up the tickets and all that."

It was Mrs Glover's habit to allow Digby the last word. Looking contented — for he had silenced her, he thought — he rolled his maps and slid them into containers. She wondered what he would say if she were to tell him this was to be her last June, and consequently their last journey abroad. She had refused the operation the doctor had offered; it seemed to her that Digby should know without having been told. But, as always, Digby was unable to see into her mind. He might not have believed what he saw; he might have supposed, with reason, that anyone able to dwell on her own death with so much distance could not believe in it either. In truth, Mrs Glover realized that she had not yet understood, and she did not believe for a moment that she would not be here, a year later, saying, "That was my last spring."

Toward the middle of June, when Janet's annual holiday began, Janet and Digby and Mrs Glover flew from London to Barcelona. At Barcelona they crossed the city by taxi and got into a bus. Janet enthusiastically recognized it as the bus she had taken on her last trip to Spain, seven years before. Mrs Glover could not remember anything about it. During the bus drive — ninety miles — Digby sat by himself. He believed himself to be desperately sick in anything moving unless he was at the wheel, and in the course of their long engagement Janet had learned not to argue. She sat beside Mrs Glover and watched the backs of Digby's ears turn dead white. He would not take anything for his indisposition, would not even eat less than usual before a trip. He refused to roll down the window so as to have a little air. He told the two women to let him alone.

Janet plainly was feeling a little squeamish herself after the bumpy air trip, but she kept up a conversation with Mrs Glover about the cycles of life. She was accustomed to thinking of older parties first, and feared that if she sat there saying nothing Mrs Glover would think her impolite.

"Every seven years a new cycle of life begins," said Janet, talking with the clarity of extreme nausea. "It is exactly seven years since you and Digby and the girls and I all met in Spain."

"Digby is being sick," said Mrs Glover.

They finished the journey in the last hour of the blazing afternoon. The heat inside the bus was stifling; the countryside was as unwelcoming as Mrs Glover remembered it. At the hotel, they parted with the speechless animosity of people who have travelled badly.

When they all three met again for dinner, Janet carried an angora stole. She declared the holiday officially open. "Oh, lovely," she said, of nothing at all. Their table in the dark dining room had been spread with perspiring tomatoes and garlic sausages. There was a bottle of brackish water, and a lump of bread apiece. Janet smiled and sat down and said, "Yes, every seven years. Digby darling, take that little bit of pepper out of the sausage, it will give you the most frightful tummy ache, especially after what happened this afternoon on the bus. When I was seven, or something *like* seven, Hitler came to power. Digby was nearly seven when his father died."

"Why doesn't he bring us some wine?" said Digby, looking round.

"Don't bother," said Janet. "I'll catch his eye. When I was fourteen — another seven years, you see — I was confirmed. By a coincidence, that was the year the war broke out. There he is.... *Vino, camarero, por favor.* Digby, I don't mind drinking that water, and I believe in drinking the water of a country, and smoking the cigarettes of a country, but I imagine your mother might want something better."

Mrs Glover could not have said just what she had been doing here seven years before. She and Digby had come into a valley, she remembered, and seen a village of white paint and stone. There was a fair, and a grove of chestnut trees, and beyond that the umbrella pines that told them they were nearing the sea. They had driven from the treeless interior, and because of the trees and the anticipation of the sea Mrs Glover had told Digby to stop. It was too late to drive on to Barcelona that night, she said, and the pleasure of waiting for the sea might be better than the truth of it, which was likely to be dirty and hot. Janet and her three office friends were in the hotel, as if waiting for Digby. They had been victims of a travel-bureau fraud. They had paid for an all-in holiday, had given up their travel allowances, and *look* at the place! Disaster made them bold enough to speak; Digby was tall and English and competent-looking. The four girls fell on his neck.

"...life," Mrs Glover suddenly heard. "At twenty-one," said Janet, tearing bread, "I had a tragic experience."

They knew. Her first lover, recovering from a broken ankle, developed pneumonia and died in a day. Seven years later, still inconsolable because unclaimed, she met the Glovers here.

"And now we are all back again, and nothing has changed," said Janet, with a fall in her voice, as if the subject had finally ended. "Nothing has changed. That's what I mean to say about life."

Nothing had changed except Janet, Mrs Glover thought. The dining room was unquestionably as it had been, and Digby was much as ever; he still fancied himself a sporting figure, his Tyrolian pullovers. As for Mrs Glover, her passion for furniture and arranging rooms had led her to resemble a piece of furniture—but had she not always? There were photographs of her taken thirty years before that a clever caricaturist could have turned into something stiff and unremarkable — a Parigiano ball-room chair.

"There is a fair, Digby," said Janet. "I saw it when we were coming into the village this afternoon. I think we might go and look at it."

Janet has changed, Mrs Glover thought. She is the only one of us who has become someone else.

At twenty-eight, Janet had worshipped Digby across the table with a look that must have been, for him, a new kind of mirror. He stared back at this image, gave orders and began showing off. Janet could stammer out only the barest facts about herself. She lived with her parents, who were vegetarians. Her father had been a clerk with a shipping line out in India. She had a job; she was not a typist or a secretary but something more important. She really ought to have been farther along than she was, she had told them, blushing steamily, but in her field all the opportunities went to men. To Mrs Glover, who knew little about jobs of any kind, it sounded astonishing, gritty and rather hot. She changed the topic and said that Digby, too, had been in India as a child.

"Ah, no, not really?" cried Janet, clasping her hands. Wasn't the world small? You met someone in Spain, in a forsaken village, and discovered you were both in India at the same time. Digby looked modest and felt praised. But Janet became silent when told that Digby's father had not been with the Army, or Shell, or anything like that, but had gone out there with his wife and son because he liked it. Liked doing what? said Janet. Why, nothing, Mrs Glover said. They liked India; that was all.

Well, Janet had heard some funny things in her life, as they were often to hear her say, but when she heard about Digby's father and mother in India for no reason to speak of, she pursed her lips as if to whistle. It *was* odd. The three girls from Janet's office seemed to agree with her. They glanced at Digby's hands to see if he hadn't a touch of coloured blood. Digby at that instant looked questioning, blunt and plain, as if the most innocent elements of parental behaviour had always been a mystery to him, too. To Digby, none of the reasons for choosing mattered; he had never heard of freedom. His mother had taken India up and put it down. She admired India, and then it fell from her personal tree and smashed to bits. Digby didn't care. What he wondered now was, what made people go to hot, dangerous places? Why should his father have died in Madras, where there was cholera, instead of dying in England, of some homely ailment, on a moist afternoon? Janet's expression gave the question form. That night, under the chestnut trees next to a fairground, Digby and Janet became engaged.

The morning after the engagement, Janet took Mrs Glover for a walk and showed her the place where she and Digby had been sitting. She indicated a rock, but Mrs Glover looked at the flattened grass beside it. "You had a pretty view," she said, pointing to the pine trees on the opposite bank. But Janet had lost her blush.

The mystery to Mrs Glover was that Digby had ever got as far as that; he was such an uninspired boy. She wondered if he had followed seduction with remorse, and asked Janet to marry him on that account. In any event, he had got no farther. Janet had brought to life, with one unbelieving expression, part of a total secret he had been wondering about for years, but he had no more questions to put; there was nothing for Janet to answer. They had never married. He lived at home with his mother, and Janet had her absorbing job. Except for one three-week holiday every summer, he and Janet seldom saw each other alone. There was no other way, was there? Not short of marriage. Janet lived with her family, Digby's mother seldom dined out, and women like Janet do not make love in doorways. It seemed to Mrs Glover, at times, that Digby had a wife in London and that Janet was a girl he took abroad.

Actually, with her clamp hold on three weeks of his life every year, Janet was about as wifelike as anything Digby had imagined. One year, having become dazzled by another girl, a jolly girl who drove an Aston Martin, he tried to put off taking Janet abroad; he hinted. Janet instantly vanished from his life, and returned his ring by registered post. It was a small diamond-and-turquoise ring that had belonged to Mrs Glover's girlhood, and she was pleased to see it again; all the same, she urged a reconciliation. She was quite certain that Janet and Digby would never marry, while the Aston Martin girl was far too lively to keep, and might be noisy about the house.

"You'd better ring Janet up, Digby," she had said.

"She doesn't expect it."

But in the end he gave in, his mother invented such a moving picture of Janet, puffy and swollen-eyed, not too far from the telephone, not too near: Janet, who had given him the best of her life, starting with twenty-eight. She described, so that it was too real to bear, Janet's mother washing the leaves of the plants with weak tea, while the father constructed a ship in a bottle. It was enough to get Digby to the telephone and urge Janet to come out of there, if only for an evening. Actually, he knew it wasn't as bad as all that; not entirely. The Crawleys lived in Putney, and ate rice, and had a garden and quite a lot of Oriental brass.

"I suppose," said Janet, with slightly more tension this

time, "we might as well go to the fair." She looked meaningfully at Digby; he ought to be helping his poor old mother up the stairs, and suggesting tactfully that she go to bed. He did nothing of the kind. He sent a waiter for his mother's wrap, and they all three set out together, as they had often done the summer of the engagement.

"It's quite a climb," said Digby, looking up at the slope and the chestnut trees and the rising lights of the fair.

"What an extraordinary moon," said Janet. "You can see everything."

Mrs Glover, possessed by pain that was now silvery and quick, now black and square, said, "Nonsense, Digby, it's no climb at all.... Yes, Janet, that is a full moon." On this hill, Digby had proposed to Janet. The lovers passed the place without remembering it, but Mrs Glover hesitated and saw the rock and remembered the grass. "But where are the pines?" she said. "Those beautiful pine trees." There was no answer; the others had gone on.

Upon a raised platform, couples from the village shuffled and stared. The orchestra consisted of one accordion, one drummer, one horn. Nearby was a life-size cardboard bull, before which one could be photographed. "Fancy," said Janet vaguely, as if she were trying to see herself and Digby and Mrs Glover having their picture taken with the bull. Mrs Glover imagined it clearly, and walked on. "Be careful, you two," said Janet, for her attention was held by the booths and the dancers, and she feared that the Glovers, without her constant solicitude, might come to grief.

Digby was increasingly fretful. In India, when he had been a funny, jaundiced-looking little boy, his mother had taken him to a fair in the hills where jewels were piled in sea shells; there had been shells of sapphires and emeralds and a large shell full of pearls. One pearl was like the moon. "I want that one," Digby said, and she had replied, "You shall have it," meaning that one got what one wanted out of life.

"Take care, you two," came Janet's voice. She had stopped now to examine the treasures offered in a stall — paperweight guitars, and sombrero ashtrays. She looked gravely at them, considering. Digby wore an expression Mrs Glover remembered from his childhood. It meant "I am going to be very naughty now." Poor boy, thought Mrs Glover, and she took his arm. I never understood that you meant what you said about the pearl, and I never said what I meant; is it any wonder you have grown puzzled? ...She might have told him, "Digby, they say I am dying, and you must marry Janet for the sake of the house," and that would have been saying what she meant, for once, but just then she heard him mutter that it had been a mistake, coming here.

"You're tired," he said.

"I'm not!"

"Well, you're not enjoying it."

"Perhaps Janet is." She looked around, but Janet was lost. "Digby," she said, "see if you can find Janet. I shall be there," she said, pointing, "you see, between the fairground and those pine trees." For that hadn't been the rock, of course; she had been mistaken. The proposal had taken place on this side of the fairground. "I shall sit down on the first rock I come to, and I shall wait. Bring Janet when you find her, and we can all go back. I don't think we're liking Spain."

"You might be cold," he protested. Had he always been this concerned? She sat down, after he had left her, not far from the place where Janet had held out her hand and said "Digby asked me to marry him there." The fair and the chestnut trees were behind her; the pine trees held out their weighted branches on the opposite slope. They no longer gave their promise of the sea. She saw them in the summer moonlight, stripped to the bark, hung with thousands, no, millions, of white cocoons. There, she thought, as if it had never occurred to her until now; everything dies.

That night she dreamed the dream that was becoming a common landscape now. It was a long Galsworthy- or Walpole-like family tale, in which Mrs Glover was not herself at all but a thin, dark-haired girl named Amabel. As Amabel, she journeyed with a young mother, four or five sisters, a governess and a butler to spend long, sunny holidays beside the sea. She saw the bright rooms of the house, breathed the sea air, touched cups and curtains sticky with it, shook jellyfish out of her bathing costume, saw the morning sun in squares on the bedroom walls, smelled her dream sisters' salty young hair on the pillows. And she knew, waking, that she was being drugged and softened and prepared by this dream so that she would go, without fighting, into oblivion, and she knew that, one night, on a journey as Amabel, with the mother and the pastel sisters and a charming young butler, she would die in her sleep.

Ah, but she had no desire to die that way; not, at least, until she was forearmed. The pleasure of the repeated dream must be stopped; for supposing she did dissolve into Amabel, and then from Amabel into someone else? She would no longer remember the worry of having once been Mrs Glover, but that still left Digby and the unsolved problem of the house. Those promises from beyond the grave, she thought, the world was full of them: small, tinny reverberations, the only immortality one could trust.

When she descended in the morning, she found Janet in the dining room. Janet said she had hardly slept a wink. She was hot-eyed but calm. Digby had not returned to her at the fair. He had vanished among the dancers. Janet had finally come home alone, and then sat and waited in her room, where she had eventually fallen asleep in a chair. Now she had been sitting hours in the hot, fly-buzzing dining room, drinking foul coffee and making inquiries. She learned that Digby had come in at four o'clock this morning dragging a cardboard bull. The bull was there, behind them; the waiters pointed to it. Instead of looking, Janet took on the high voice of command and ordered Mrs Glover's breakfast. Protein makes up for lost sleep; she sent up a second breakfast for Digby, with plenty of bacon and a soft-boiled egg.

"Janet, my dear, I'm afraid I lost you, too. I spent some time looking for the pine trees, and then when I saw them they were dead."

"I know," said Janet. "I saw them, too." She leaned her head against her hand, in a pose of classical melancholy. She said, in a tired voice, "They are something called processional caterpillars. They kill everything, but I don't believe they ever become anything much—just a little browny sort of moth. I have to know a little bit about that. You know, it's my job." As though something of the most excruciating intimacy had been said, she turned red—the blush she had lost with her long engagement.

No, Mrs Glover did not know; but she knew there is control from beyond the grave, if one is careful to establish it in time. Janet must marry Digby because Digby was unfit to stay alone, and because Janet must learn to take care of the house, the pictures, the rugs, the tables, the knives and the forks, the glasses and chairs. Mrs Glover's unwelcome death must be provided for; Janet must be given time to learn.

"Digby is restless," said Mrs Glover.

This was the first time they had ever mentioned Digby in his absence, and Janet sat quite still. She looked at the stains on the table-cloth and the flies devouring crumbs. She said, "I'm devoted to Digby, of course."

"Devoted" was as much as Mrs Glover was likely to get. Janet might adore her own mother, or a fine day, or a pretty tune, but she would never be more than devoted to a lover. Mrs Glover understood it, and was grateful. Understatement made it possible to be both sensible and cruel, and since living often obliged one to be both, it gave the assurance that no one would be harmed too deeply. She was grateful to Janet for being devoted and nothing more.

"I am devoted to Digby," Janet went on, playing with crumbs, "but last night has changed things. If he's going to be that sort, coming in drunk and that, I don't want him."

Mrs Glover wasted no time thinking this was not true. She saw the tight lines around Janet's mouth; the wretched woman was hopelessly moral where marriage was concerned. She would trail on in an endless engagement as long as Digby wanted, probably accepting some peevish story of mother love, only man of the family, mother would perish; but she would not marry a man who could desert his mother and his betrothed at a public fair in a foreign country and come in at four o'clock in the morning with a cardboard bull. That was the lucky thing about a long engagement, she could almost hear Janet say — it gave you time to find every possibility out.

"Digby is slightly restless, and marriage would settle him," said Mrs Glover, pitying Digby, who now joined the company of men whose fate had been settled by a pair of women over empty cups.

"It's changed things," said Janet again. "I shall have to think about it now."

"Perhaps there isn't much time," said Mrs Glover.

"Oh, there's plenty of that," said Janet sadly, as though nothing but time were left.

THE HUNTER'S
WAKING THOUGHTS

❖

❖

BETWEEN Friday night and Saturday noon, the court-yard filled with cars and station wagons, lined up like animals feeding along the wall of the hunting lodge. The license plates were mostly 75s, from Paris, but some of the numbers meant Lyon and one was as far away from Sologne as Avignon. Across the court, under the oak trees, the dogs, each chained to his kennel, barked insanely. Only two of the shooting party had brought dogs; the twelve chained dogs belonged to M Maitrepierre, who had let the shooting rights to his estate for the season. Walking under the oak trees to have a better look at the dogs, the men in their boots trod on acorns and snails. The men were stout and middle-aged but dressed like the slimmer, handsomer models in *Adam*. A recent issue of *Adam*, advising a wardrobe for the hunting season, was on the window sill of the dining room reserved for the party. There was also *Entreprise*, a business journal, and several copies of *Tintin*.

The hunters slammed doors the whole morning and carried bushels of equipment from the cars to the lodge. M Scapa, a repatriated *pied-noir* from Algiers, had brought a chauffeur to look after his guns, his own case of whiskey, and his plaid-covered ice bucket. The lodge was ugly and awkward and had been built two hundred years after the other buildings on the estate. The big house was sold. M Maitrepierre reserved for himself, his wife, and his married daughter and her family a cottage separated from the lodge by a locked gate and a wall. The shooting rights, which were high, were not his only source of income; he ran a sheep farm and half a dozen of the secret French

113

economic tangles that come to light during family squab-
bles or taxation lawsuits. He built blocks of flats in Paris,
sold a hotel in Normandy, bought part of a clothing factory
in Lille. He kept his family tamed by the threat that they
were doomed and bankrupt and on the verge of singing for
their supper on some rainy street.

The shooting season had been open for over a month, but
game was still so plentiful here in Sologne that pheasants,
with their suicidal curiosity about automobiles, stood along
the roads. Small hunter-coloured couples, they were paro-
dies of hunters. Anyone gathering mushrooms or chestnuts
raised pheasant and quail. In pastures the hind legs of hares
were glimpsed in the long grass. Saturdays and Sundays the
farmers tied their dogs and kept the children inside, for the
men who arrived in the big cars with the smart equipment
shot without aiming; they shot at anything. A man wearing
a suede jacket had been mistaken for a deer and wounded
in the shoulder. There were any number of shot cats, turkeys
and ducks. Every season someone told of a punctured sheep.
Casual poachers who left their cars drawn up on the edge
of the highway came back to find a hole in the windshield
and a web of cracked glass.

This was flat country in a season of rich colours — brown,
dark red, gold.

Colin Graves, who was in love with M Maitrepierre's
married daughter, Nathalie, and younger than she was by
nine years, had been put in the lodge. The lodge smelled
like a school. Colin had not come to shoot but to be near
Nathalie. Now that he was here, and saw that he was to
sleep in the lodge, and that Nathalie's husband had arrived,
he wondered if there had been a mistake — if he had turned
up on the wrong weekend. The hunters strode and stamped,
carrying whiskey glasses. The wooden stairs shook under
their boots. Some went out on Saturday afternoon, but most

of the party waited for Sunday morning. They ate enormous meals. They neither washed nor shaved. It was part of the ritual of being away from their women.

Colin had been given a room with a camp bed and a lamp and a ewer of cold water, and a bucket with an enamel cover. Nathalie showed him the room and let him start to undress her on the bed before changing her mind. She worried about what the family would think — so she said — and she left him there, furious and demented. Was it because of the husband? No, she swore the husband had nothing to do with it. She talked rapidly, fastening her cardigan. Nothing went on between Nathalie and the husband. It had gone wrong years ago. Well, one year ago, at least. The husband's room in the lodge was next to Colin's. Nathalie was to spend the night in her own girlhood bed, in her father's house. What other evidence did Colin want?

He was the only foreigner here. He was a bad shot, and loathed killing. He supposed that everyone looked at him and guessed his situation. Why was he here? She had invited him; but she had not told him her husband was coming, too, or that she would be sleeping in another house. They were an odd couple. Colin was slight and fair. He was in Paris, translating Jules Renard's letters. He had met Nathalie because it was through one of her father's multitudinous enterprises he had found a place to live. Nathalie was Spanish-looking, and rather fat since the birth of her second daughter. Colin loved her beyond reason and cherished dreams in which the husband, the two little girls and Nathalie's own common sense about money were somehow mislaid.

On Sunday morning, he walked with a party of women. There were three: Nathalie, her mother and Nathalie's closest woman friend. If he included Nathalie's little girls, he had five females in all. The lover trailed behind the women, peevish as a child. They were walking far from the shooting party, on the shore of a shallow pond. Along the path he saw a snail and trod on it, afterward wiping his shoe on fallen leaves. Most galling to him was the way the women admired Nathalie; there was no mistaking the admiration in their eyes. She was bringing off a situation they could only applaud; she was getting away with murder. She had put her husband and her lover in adjacent rooms while she slept in calm privacy in her father's house. Now here she was, fat and placid, with the lover tagging like a spaniel. What was the good of keeping slim, starving oneself, paying out fortunes to be smart, when fat Nathalie could keep two men on the string without half trying? Colin saw this in the other women's eyes.

He knew they thought she was his mother; but the maternal part of her life disgusted him. The idea of her having ever been a mother — the confirmation, the two girls, ran along before the women (Colin was like one of the women now!)made him sick. Early that morning,Nathalie's father had taken Colin on a tour of the sheep farm, and at the sight of a lambing chart on the wall of a pen — a pen called *le nursery* — Colin had been puzzled by the diagram of a lamb blind and doubled up in a kind of labyrinth. His mind first told him, "Surrealistic drawing"; then he realized what it was and was revolted. The thought of Nathalie on a level with animals — ewes, bitches, mares — was unbearable. He could not decide if he wanted her as a woman or a goddess. When he returned from the sheep pens, he found that Nathalie, meanwhile, had been attending to her husband — unpacking for him, and giving him breakfast.

The children, the women, and Colin walked along the edge of the pond, and separated the strands of barbed wire that marked someone else's property. Before them, at the end of a long terrace, among oak and acacia trees, rose a shuttered house. It was an ugly and pretentious house, built fifty years ago, imitating without grace a deeper past. He saw the women admiring it, and Nathalie yearning for it — for a large, shuttered, empty, pretentious house. Nathalie was already seeing what she would "do" to the place. She described the tubs of hydrangeas along the façade and the wrought-iron baskets dripping with geraniums. He pressed her arm as if afraid. What will become of us? What will happen if we quarrel?

The two women, Nathalie's mother and Nathalie's best friend, were as kind to Colin as if he were a dog. He felt the justice of it. He had the dog's fear of being left behind. He was like the dog shut up in the automobile who has no means of knowing his owner will ever return. He had seen dogs' eyes yellow with anxiety.... The most abject of lovers can be saved by pride. He dropped her arm, made her sense he was moving away. It was no accident he had chosen as a subject of work conceited Jules Renard. The hideous house belonged to a broker who had fumbled or gone crooked on a speculation, but (explained Nathalie) luckily had this place to fall back on. He seldom lived in the house, but he *owned* it. It was his; it was real. He knew it was there. Nathalie could admire story-book castles, but she never wanted them. Story-book castles were what Colin wanted her to want, because they were all he could give her. He hadn't a penny. She was waiting for an inheritance from her father, and another from her mother. Her husband hadn't quite gone through her marriage settlement; not yet.

Nathalie stuffed her pockets with acorns and cracked them with her teeth. She was always making motions of eating, of biting. She bit acorns, chestnuts, twigs. She was solid as this house, and solidity was what she wanted: something safe, something she could fall back on. She spat a chewed acorn out of her mouth into her palm. "You're too young to remember the war, Colin," she said, smiling at him. "We used to make coffee out of these filthy things."

Sunday night the bag was divided, the courtyard slowly rid of its cars. Colin, earlier, had walked around the *tableau de chasse*, the still life spread on the ground, pretending admiration. He saw hares so riddled they would never be clean of shot. He was sick for the larks. He was to spend Sunday night at the cottage, with Nathalie's father and mother. Her father would drive him up to Paris on Monday morning. He was to sleep in Nathalie's girlhood bed. His sheets had been thriftily moved from the lodge and carried the smell of the unwashed house. Nathalie's husband all at once wanted to be in Paris. He wanted to pack the car and leave now. The weekend was over; there was no reason to remain another second. Fat and placid Nathalie screamed at him, "You have imposed a dinner party on me for tomorrow night. Now, take your choice. We leave now, this minute, and you take tomorrow's guests to a restaurant. Or you wait until the game is divided and we have a hare." The family were not entitled to any of the game, except by courtesy. Nathalie's husband had gone out with the shooting party, but he had not paid his share of the shooting rights on his father-in-law's property; he had no claim to so much as a dead thrush.

"You can't cook a freshly killed hare," said Nathalie's mother.

Everyone else kept out of it.

"He knows the butchers are closed on Mondays, and he knows I have an incompetent Spanish maid, and thrusts a Monday-night dinner party on me," cried Nathalie. The husband, black with temper, read *Tintin*. The little girls played dominoes on a corner of a table. Colin watched Nathalie without being noticed. If he had laid a hand on her now, she might have hit him.

She left, at last, with the token hare in a basket. Nathalie's mother's voice wailed after the car, "Nathalie! Nathalie! The hare should marinate at least twelve days!" She returned to the cottage and saw her daughter's guest, the lover, standing in the middle of the room. "My son-in-law is indescribable," she said. "My daughter is a saint. Have you enjoyed the weekend, Colin? Do you like the country, or do you like cities better? Would you like a drink?"

Her husband, Nathalie's father, had gone, flashlight in hand, to the hunting lodge, to recover anything left by the party: dregs of whiskey in open bottles, half-crumbled chocolate bars.

"How sensible you are not to marry," said Nathalie's mother, sitting down. "The world would be simpler if women lived with women and men with men. I don't mean anything perverse. But look at how peaceful we were without the men today." They had their drinks, and Colin crawled into his sheets, in his mistress's girlhood bed. It was then he started to wonder if he shouldn't look for someone to marry after all.

CARELESS TALK

❖

❖

THEIR language — English — drew them together. So did their condition in a world they believed intended for men. They were Iris Drouin, the London girl inexplicably married to a French farmer (inexplicably only because other people's desires are so strange), and Mary Olcott, her summer neighbour and friend. On a June night Mary had suddenly appeared in the Drouins' kitchen doorway while the family were at their meal. She was Irish and twenty-seven, with the manner of a Frenchwoman of forty — foxy and Parisian in her country clothes. She was a shade too sure of herself; it went down badly in this corner of Burgundy, where summer visitors were disliked. Lounging in the doorway, letting in mosquitoes and moths, Mary addressed the men — Iris's young husband and her old father-in-law — but her wide smile was for Iris as well. The two men went on shovelling boiled beef.

"Please don't get up," said Mary — as if they meant to! "I am Mme Olcott, your new neighbour. I've rented the pink house — I'm sure you know. News travels so fast in these places. I should like to buy my milk and eggs from you now."

She had created the Drouins Providers by Appointment, but the men's faces said she had something to learn. Mary was a woman; it was up to another woman to put her down. And so Iris, the Cockney stray, sick with shyness, hugely pregnant with her first child, had to answer, "We don't sell in small quantities. Everything goes to the co-operative. You can buy your milk in the village."

When Iris talked French her mouth was full of iron filings; that was how it sounded and felt. Mary caught the accent and cried in English, "Oh, how marvellous! Even if you won't sell me milk, let me come over and talk to you sometimes. I miss English." Her hand in the pocket of her suede coat might have held a stone. Iris had a queer reaction of fright. She looked first at the two men, as if seeking permission, then back at Mary. Their eyes met, as women's seldom do at a first encounter.

Mary won, of course. From that evening on she bought milk, eggs, butter, honey and cheese at the farm. She came and went like a chatelaine, and nothing heralded her approach; not the bell at the gate, not even the dogs. Iris thought sometimes that Mary had power over animals but was not aware of it, and did not know she was almost a witch.

"The first time I saw you, you were like a character in 'Goupi-Mains Rouges,'" Mary said to Iris about a year later. "None of you spoke. I remember the bare petrol lamp on the table. The stars were so thick I could see the dogs sleeping when I crossed the courtyard. In the kitchen, you looked evil and wicked, as if you were hiding a bag of gold or a corpse. Suddenly there *you* were, an honest London sparrow chirping away."

Iris had thought, She's like the queen of spades.

Since her marriage, Iris had lived where nothing changed except the weather, yet everything seemed out of joint. No homely object was like any she had seen; a chair was not a chair now, because it was *une chaise*. This was particular, personal; no one could know what it was like. She sensed at the beginning that her stylish new neighbour would never mind her own business. Most Frenchwomen minded that above everything else. Then Mary said something in English, and was therefore safe. Iris had married into a life she had not expected, and safety came down to language now. French was quicksand and English the rock.

She went into friendship without caution, without posting mutual bail. Mary gave her something she missed to the point of illness: a language that made sense. During the winter, when Mary's pink house was shuttered and Mary's existence assured by the rolled-up English papers she posted from Paris — papers that Iris hadn't time to open, let alone read — Iris lived on stored talk. She heard Mary's voice, and she thought she heard her own. The topics never varied; there wasn't a second to spare for casual chatter. Iris had work to do, and Mary was pulled by a private life. Iris talked about time, and how time changed your view, like a turn in the road. She talked about money; surely money was freedom? She talked about women's lives. Women's lives could be bent like wire in the hands of men. Iris didn't care what was said about modern women in a modern world; she had seen her mother's life and now she was living her own.

Mary agreed about time, which was abstract, and was vague about money; she had nearly all she needed of both. But men, now! "Ah, don't get me started," she would beg, and sometimes Iris was sorry she had started, for her friend became a bird in a room, blundering against the walls, too frantic to see the door. Not that Mary Olcott was a bird; she was dark, with a legend of dark women behind her. She had the whole village in her pocket from the first summer on. Iris was a little jealous of that. From her height Mary looked down on lesser lives, giving bad marks or, worse, none at all. Marcel, Iris's husband, fled like a hare at the sight of Mary. From a distance he said, *"Très américaine."* In the village they said, *"Très anglaise."* She was neither; her parents had come over from Ireland in the early twenties, and Mary was born some ten years later. It was the only fact she ever told. Iris thought that even if she were to live in the pink brick house with Mary, listen to her telephone conversations, look at the postmarks on her envelopes, she would still never know more.

For two summers Mary Olcott rented the house next to the Drouins' farm, and the third summer bought it. In the village it was said that a married lawyer, Parisian, had made her a present of it. Iris never listened to gossip. It was enough, for her, to have Mary nearby from June to October. The pink house was in sight of Iris's bedroom. Pinning back her hair at dawn (she never had time for a mirror), Iris saw the shaded windows and the west lawn, with the rose garden still asleep. The house was surrounded by the Drouins' fields on three sides. The Drouin men knew to a centimetre where the boundaries stopped, and they encroached upon Mary, inch by inch, every season. The two houses were six miles from the village, which was as far as Iris travelled, and about two and a half hours from Paris — on weekdays an easy drive.

Mary went up to Paris often. She seemed to like the country as a setting, but the threat of rain was enough to chase her away. Now, three years after the first meeting in the Drouins' kitchen, this is how matters were. Mary was Iris's only friend, and Iris was Mary's when Mary happened to be down at the country place.

Mary Olcott's pleasure was collecting confidences, not giving them out. She had a talent for friendship, or, rather, for taming people. The more shy and resistant they seemed, the more she displayed her charm, her strength and her sense of timing. She hunted the cautious person whose sudden unguarded word or gesture gave a secret away. Dozens of women had said to her, "You are my only friend." She had exclusive friendship for each of them. She played simultaneous chess games, ten at a time. The conquest of Iris (and the collateral defeat of two men, Drouin father and son, who had tried to refuse to sell Mary eggs and milk) had not been as complete as it appeared. During the winter, when Mary was away, she forgot what Iris was like. She had

any number of Irises to take up her time. She sent magazines and papers because she hated throwing anything
away. At their first meeting, until Iris spoke, Mary had
thought, She could be the old man's wife. Then Iris's
dreadful accent gave the question depth, like more and more
gauze curtains going up. Mary found hardest to place, in
the first minute, Iris's wizened dowdiness, as if it were a
disease that must inevitably follow first youth. Later, Mary
changed her mind a hundred times. Iris was simple, yes,
but not so simple as all that. She clung to Mary as though
she were sinking, but sometimes of her own accord Iris let
go the boat, and Mary never knew why. Iris was cold; she
cried and laughed like a Latin. She worked. She was dis-
organized, lazy, slack. Here Mary thought a word she had
not used for years — "slack." Iris's teeth were going. One day
soon, she would have no age at all; but she was younger
than Mary by three or four years. She wept for English,
but when her two babies were born she talked to them in
French. Marcel did not want his children to be strangers
— that was the reason Iris gave. Iris had always felt like Iris,
never doubted what being Iris meant, until now, talking
French to her own children.

"He only suggested it, but it was really an order. Sometimes I don't feel like myself at all."

Iris could say this to Mary without a preliminary statement, picking up an idea dropped last Wednesday, Thursday, any day. She could say anything. Iris and Mary were
an island, an English fortress, here in hostile France. She
said anything to Mary without wondering how far it would
go. It was a triumph for Mary, but she had to remember
never to be too sure of herself; she never knew when Iris
would open her hands and let go the boat.

This was Friday morning and Mary's next-to-last weekend for the season. She stood in the kitchen doorway with
a heavy grey sky behind her. An Italian basket dangled from

her hand; she had come for the eggs or cheese for that day's lunch. Really, she had come to talk to Iris. Iris's babies played on the stone floor, among piles of dirty clothes sorted for the wash. They saw the visitor, but Iris didn't. The kitchen was full of steam and noise. Because the second child was a son, Marcel had brought electricity into the kitchen and made his wife a present of a water heater and a second-hand washing machine. The machine was a tub on stilt legs. It made a sound like a battering-ram and in motion rocked the house. Iris sensed her visitor, felt the presence in the doorway, and turned off the machine. The noise died, and she held out her hands, smiling, happy to see her friend.

"Mary, look at my hands," she said. "Just look at them. They look like boiled lobster. Do you know, my mother made my bed and darned for me and washed my things until the day I was married? My mother said, 'Have a good time while you can.' She said, 'When a man gets hold of you, you'll work enough for him.'"

"True," said Mary Olcott, who had never worked for anybody. "But you must have wanted this life. Otherwise you wouldn't have chosen Marcel."

She's in *that* mood, Iris thought.

Mary's profile was cold, her black hair drawn back over her ears. She was too strong; no one could live up to the standards she set for her friends. No wonder she frightened Marcel! In the silence of the kitchen Iris thought, She doesn't frighten me.

Curled by the steam in the room, Iris's thin hair looked sculptured. The curl had been induced by a packaged home perm her mother sent from England. Relief parcels kept Iris in touch; her frocks and the children's toys were Marks & Spencer. Her wedding picture — an English bride in a chromium frame — stood on a shelf above the washing machine. Marcel had been made to go to England for his wedding,

but it was his only trip abroad. On his sole seaside holiday he had met Iris, and his marriage involved a journey,
too. He did not see why he should go beyond the village
again.

"*Bonjour,*" said Mary gravely to the blond dirty babies,
aged two and one. The second was her godson.

"I mind mostly that they'll never have English nursery
rhymes and English songs," said Iris. "They'll never know
my rhymes."

"That was the sacrifice you made when you married a
stranger," Mary said.

"It wasn't a sacrifice," Iris said passionately, pleading for
justice.

"You weren't a girl of seventeen."

"No, but I was so ignorant. I thought I knew it all, but I
was ignorant."

This great confidence Mary accepted as her due. She was
the rock on which weaker natures broke. She saw their
hopes and failings turned back like waves. Hard, lucid, tire-
lessly inquisitive, her eyes looked beyond Iris, measuring
Iris. She seemed totally just.

"You can be mistaken about a kind of life without being
mistaken about the person you marry," Iris said. She turned
on the washing machine so that the noise put an end to
that kind of talk, for the moment. She did not look at her
babies; they were too beautiful, too personal, too betrayed
by what she had revealed to Mary. Whatever happened,
they must never be shared. Even looking at the children
now with Mary in the doorway would have been sharing.

"My friend has arrived," Mary said.

"I saw the car."

"I said, my friend is here."

"I *know.*"

They were shouting over the battering-ram of the
machine. Their voices came back from the walls. The stones

of the house understood nothing but French; they could shout all they liked. The mud in the courtyard was French, soaked in French. Mary said something in a normal tone, unheard. Iris switched off the machine.

"...over seventy. She's marvellous. She's brought a Dominican with her. He drove her up from Bordeaux. She never goes out of the house, but when she decides to, she cruises around the country in an old, old Mercedes. With a Dominican."

"Oh. Well, very interesting, I'm sure." Iris was a Catholic convert. She had become a Catholic when she married Marcel. First she wanted to please him; then, because she brought her Protestant self along, as an act of faith she became wholly Catholic and a bigot. Mary Olcott was Catholic, but sloppy about it. She had what Iris called "views." Moreover, Iris was suspicious of the French, the social part of Mary's life — her traffic with the enemy, as it were.

Iris's "I'm sure" was quite sarcastic, but Mary missed the change in tone and went on, "She's marvellous, old Mademoiselle. Everyone in her family calls her 'Mademoiselle,' even her family — even her doddering old brothers. It's teasing, but it's a kind of homage, too. She's such an old *girl* — such a maiden. She should have been a nun at Port Royal. I can see her there, defying everyone — defying the King. She never looks at a newspaper. She doesn't know a thing about the Algerian war, except when one of her great-nephews is called up. But she reads Greek, and she taught herself Russian when she was sixty, because she wanted to read Pushkin. She's priest-ridden, though. She always has some decayed old padre around. But this one isn't old. This one is young and modern."

Iris stood, frowning, with her hand on the switch of the washing machine.

"A young Dominican," said Mary. "You'll meet him.

You'll bring the children to tea this afternoon—please. *He's* staying the night; then he goes to Paris. He is a psychologist," said Mary with light scorn. "Confessor to society women. Confessor to débutantes. 'Tell me all about it. I understand the world.' Well, I must think about their lunch. I'll have eggs, Iris, and cream if you can spare any. If you have any of your soft white cheese, I'll take a pound or so."

She's in that mood, Iris thought. She's in that mood again. She doesn't frighten me.

"We stopped in the village," said the old Frenchwoman, in her asthmatic voice. Her hair was chopped straight at the tip of the ear. She was wearing what must have been plush curtains once. "We stopped to ask directions, and also because we were early and feared it would be a bother for you, dear Mary, if we arrived before you were expecting us. We sat in a café named Chez Mémé and saw the news on television. The news is the same as when I last looked at it. Men are being chased by other men holding sticks. This salmon is perfect. I've had nothing like it in twenty years."

Mary Olcott instantly forgot she had been irritated because her friend Mademoiselle and Mademoiselle's new friend, Father Eugène, had stopped in *her* village. They had stopped so that Mademoiselle could gather gossip. The mention of perfect salmon restored her.

The young Dominican, at the head of the long table, with a woman at either hand, was clearly enjoying his lunch, but his mind was elsewhere—not far: on himself. Both Mary's guests were talkative, and each voice had a peculiarity. The old woman's was gaspy, the priest's rapid and faint. Both talked with their mouths full. Mary let them talk to each other. She fixed her attention on the yellow dahlias that were almost all that remained of the autumn garden. The hazelnut tree was dying a mysterious lingering death. The hazelnut and the dahlias were all she could see of the east lawn. The immortal acacia, which she loved superstitiously, under which they would presently meet Iris and her babies for tea, was on the west side. There, if the sun broke through as Mary wanted, they would sit and drink their tea and admire Mary's roses. Beyond the garden, surrounding Mary's house on three sides, were the Drouins' fields.

A Drouin tractor moved toward the dining room and the east lawn; it stopped, backed, turned, a few feet from the dying hazelnut tree. Perched on the tractor, dressed in boots and working clothes, was the village priest.

The young Dominican in his creamy robes said, "In Professor Thibeault's group I wore lay clothes and did not say I was a priest. I was afraid it would make the patients afraid."

"You were spying," gasped Mademoiselle.

"I was learning. Group therapy."

"Spying," the old woman said.

"In that group was a teacher of mathematics, a Stendhal expert, a Jew and two homosexuals," said Father Eugène. "After four sessions they discovered I was a priest and were dismayed. I spoke about troubles of my own, so that they would go on. Otherwise they would have frozen. They would have frozen first of all because I am a priest, and secondly," said the young man, with composure, "because I am not a neurotic."

At every wicked word the old woman looked briefly at the ceiling. It just might fall.

"But you *were* spying," said Mary, who always ate less than anyone else and had time to listen, elbows on the table, her chin in her hands. "You were a spy and the psychiatrist was your accomplice. Isn't that so?"

Father Eugène stared through horn-rimmed spectacles as round as his boyish face. He laid his knife and fork down with care. He had not suppressed his personality but could behave as if he had. "I was studying, and had been sent there for that purpose," he said. He was accustomed to arousing spitefulness and even hate in some women, just as he accepted being fawned upon by others. Unless the reaction was deeply interesting and unexpected, he did not pursue the cause. Father Eugène and Mary Olcott had no time for each other. Whatever she had to tell she would not say to him; and he would most certainly not confide in her. They were rival talkers; more important, and fatal for the harmony of the party, they were also rival listeners.

"You have no right to have any problems," the old woman told him. "I don't see what problems you can have. You are fed and clothed. Everyone admires and respects you. Nothing costs you a speck of dust in love or duty, because your life is a sacrifice and you wanted it that way. If I had a son, I would want him to be exactly like you. As for *our* so-called problems, or the problems of those unfortunate maniacs, who seem to talk such a lot, they are *not* your affair. You are the director of my conscience, but you have no right to search my mind. It is undignified and unfair."

"But that isn't fair, either," said Mary eagerly. "You can't just say what you want to say and leave the rest dark. There is more to confession than sin. If you won't give up voluntarily, it is his right to search."

He glanced at her. So you are on our side, are you?

Oh, no, she stared at him. Make no mistake about me. I am not.

"Our Father in Heaven knows what He wants," said Mademoiselle, suddenly very coy. "So did my father. What a tyrant! And so Father Eugène must know what he is doing, too." And she gave him a look as coy as a little girl's. She had remembered that he was a representative of her father, or her Father, and she was as silly as a girl. Mary had never seen her silly. She had seen Mademoiselle with tatty hangdog priests she could bully; but Father Eugène, who could have been her grandchild, was promoted several generations on. How can she be such a ninny, Mary wondered. Mademoiselle had a brain; she read Greek and learned Russian, alone, when she was past sixty. Her books were sent to her from Russia — a Tolstoy fantasy country that had nothing to do with the real world. She had not looked at a newspaper for years. Yet she was quick when it came to saving money; she soon found out that Russian books cost less if they came straight from Russia. She knew all about filling in forms, and the name of the export office in Moscow. The books, the beautiful alphabet on harsh paper, sternly bound, came from a soft-focus grassy place where young girls wearing exquisite frocks played croquet.

Mademoiselle wore old plush curtains and kept scraps of cloth — scarves, of a sort — to spread on her head when she felt a draft. She could feel a window open in a pantry when she sat knitting five rooms away. When she was not reading, she knitted. In the old days, her knitting had gone straight to Africa. Now it appeared that the Africans were getting their hot clothing somewhere else. There was no longer the same demand. The nuns had told her so, without explaining why. She sent bundles of garments to her young friend Mary Olcott, begging her to distribute them among the poor. Every so often Mary undid a parcel from Mademoiselle and found a pullover for a swan, a bathing suit for an octopus. The knitting was large and loose as a child's, full of knots.

Mademoiselle was coy with the young priest, promoting him to super-paternity, but she had the last word. After lunch, when he blessed the women, she barely let him finish before saying, "You may direct my conscience, but it stops there. Don't you dare pry into my mind."

Late in the afternoon, the neighbouring farmer's children were brought to tea. The Drouin babies were like *putti* and a local sight, outdoing the oak tree, said to be a thousand years old, near the village. The sun had come out, as Mary expected. They sat on the west lawn. The old closed-in courtyard had been here when the house was a farm. Now the outbuildings were torn down and replaced by low soft-pink brick walls. There was Mary's acacia and the rose garden, and a view of the Drouin fields. The brown, green, blue and pink of medieval miniatures were perfectly proportioned here, although the blue of the real sky was on top instead of the rose of heaven — Mary pointed this out.

"Earth, water, fire and air are the only Christian symbols I need," said Mary, settling her guests in basket chairs. "And the acacia, because it never dies. This is why I wanted the house." A slight insistence on "wanted" did not escape one of the guests, and implied that the house had, perhaps, been a present.

Mademoiselle had slept for two hours and was knitting now, drawing up an endless thread of ugly yellow from a basket at her feet. To the two French visitors, the west lawn was a wretched room without a ceiling. The autumn sun was cold. They would have appreciated the rose garden just as well framed by curtains and cut up in squares.

Iris, in a sleeveless English print dress, sat on the grass, with her babies nearby. They were washed and pink, and their hair was like silk. Mademoiselle looked at them and said, "They are beautiful children," and "They look foreign," as if each remark were of equal value, and worth about a glass of water. She pointed her needle and the flag of knitting to the field where a tractor came and went. The tractor had followed Mary's party; it had threatened the dining room, and now rattled and roared on the west side of the house. "I understand the village priest works for you," said Mademoiselle.

"He's our best worker," said Iris.

"Aren't you impressed, having your *curé* on the tractor?"

"Glad, not impressed," said the English girl. "He's the best worker we have."

"I should be intimidated," said the old woman.

The English girl flushed and raised her voice. "Why? He likes the work. He's a farmer, the son of a farmer." She broke off, as if she had discussed all this before. She went on in a lower tone. "He's obliged to work, and that's all wrong. You should see the collection at church. Centimes. People have the nerve to leave centimes. Rich Parisians here for the summer. Summer people with big cars. They ought to be ashamed."

"The farmers are discontented," said the old woman placidly. "It was explained on the television Chez Mémé this morning. Also Father Eugène and I read their propaganda posters along the roads."

"Do you think it's right that a bottle of mineral water costs more than a bottle of milk?" said Iris, looking up, grass in her hand pulled by the roots. "All they have to do with water is put it in bottles. For milk you need cows and what every cow represents as an investment — you don't know what it represents."

"It is absolutely incorrect — " began Father Eugène, but he never finished; they never knew whose side he was on. The women gave him a look of bitter surprise. He kept his social comment to himself. Undisturbed, he watched the receding tractor. The acacia seemed a poverty-stricken tree, and despite his hostess's medieval faith, its mortality was proven. He was spending the night and going on to Paris in the morning, leaving Mademoiselle, who had nagged him. The countryside was outside his province; it was neither a complex personality nor a work of art.

"How did you know the *curé* was on the tractor?" said Mary. "What a lot of information you picked up on the television Chez Mémé!" She wanted Iris to know she had not been tattling about the village priest. But she had talked, more than a little, about Iris's curious marriage: how lost the London girl was here, how her father-in-law bullied her. She had told it as an interesting story, but now the story had substance, because Iris was here.

Iris pulled grass as if it were enemy hair. Mary must have made a good thing of the parish priest working for Marcel, but Mary was betraying her in any case, just by having these strange friends and speaking perfect French to them. Because they were foreigners, Iris did not grade them on the English staircase. They were all dangerous and all the same. Mary had no class awareness, but that seemed to Iris a handicap, like an inability to tell the time. Mary ought to have been born a snob, and her not seeming one made Iris uneasy. Yes, thought Iris, she has the farmer's wife to tea, and I sit on the grass; but she would think it normal to have me or that old lady or the Dominican washing up afterward in the kitchen, and that is where Mary makes one unsteady....And so Iris seemed anxious, suddenly; looked to see where the babies had got to—they were not far. She remembered how much she loved them, and that none of these three had children —not Mary, who would not say what she had done with her husband or who had given her the house; or the old woman; or the clever priest. The old woman went on knitting, as if to prove she could do one thing women usually did well.

Iris got up, abruptly, and shook hands all round, as she had learned to do over here. The Dominican laid his hand in hers as if confiding it.

"I must see Marcel," said Iris. "He might want something. He might be hungry."

"It's not his suppertime," said Mary idly. "Can't he wait?"

"Why should he? Besides, I've scarcely seen him the whole day."

The look on her listeners' faces was fleeting but odd. What had Mary told them, Iris wondered. As rudely as possible, she turned and walked away.

Father Eugène and Mademoiselle saw no reason to remain outside a second longer. They returned to the house and sat down on each side of an empty fireplace. Mary saw Iris as far as the road. Iris's face was stubborn and closed. She had dropped away; she would sink and drown, but she would not be cheated. No use asking her what had gone wrong, for the moment. Mary wondered if something careless had been said.

In the house, she found Mademoiselle beside the cold hearth and was told that Father Eugène had gone up to his room. He had had enough of them, too, Mary supposed. Perhaps Iris had bored him. Why read too much into it? He might have wanted to write a letter or say a prayer. She sat in his chair. She looked cold and pure and was wildly worried. Judgment Day had not been this afternoon, but it was always closer.

"What a nice girl that farmer's wife seems to be," said Mademoiselle, knitting violently. "In the village, they say she is a convert and exceptionally devout."

"Converts have it soft," said Mary. "They come to it late, without ever having had the Devil under the bed. They sail in and admire the stained-glass windows. All the dirty work has been done."

"You don't like converts, and I see you don't care for Father Eugène." Mademoiselle employed a tone suitable for an underpaid, overworked and complaining servant. "The Church is the Church. You are always free to go."

"You know I am not."

Mademoiselle put a scarf on her head and wound the

ends around her throat, but still Mary did nothing about the fire.

"I shall have nightmares tonight," said Mary. "I think it was all his talk at lunch. The mad Stendhal expert — can you see him? You may be right....I don't like them, not really. They put our dogs down a well."

"Who?"

"Young seminarists. In Ireland. Over politics. Our two spaniels. Just for the pleasure of watching them struggle and drown. Clawing the sides."

"You saw this?"

"No, it was years before I was born. I heard the story so often."

"You must never imagine things you've never seen. It is far worse to imagine cruelty than watch it. It seems to me wicked to fill your mind with horrible things you never saw. The dogs may not have scratched the sides of the well at all. They may have gone down like stones. Like the sad dog in one of my dear Turgenev's stories. You are imagining cruelty. I must say, I am surprised in a woman as charitable as you."

"I don't trust any of them," said Mary. "That's the truth. Men in skirts."

"What about men in aprons? Freemasons! A skirt has more dignity. Besides, Father Eugène would never drown a dog. He doesn't notice animals."

"I don't trust any of them." It took in a wider clan than priests.

"Life is so different now," said the old lady. "All this constant talk. 'That's what I don't like,' Oblomov said, 'Everyone talking.' " With the unpredictable jumps of the aged, she said, "When I was a child I never looked into a mirror. We were four sisters and none of us ever looked at her own face. We weren't taught it was wrong, but simply unworthy. Coquetry was beneath us. Nowadays, my nieces and their daughters..."

Mary Olcott must often look in the mirror. The perfectly smooth and glossy hair required staring—concentrated staring.

"I shall have nightmares," said Mary. "I'm sure of it. The mad Stendhal expert! But Father Eugène will sleep."

"Why shouldn't he?" said the old lady. "He is a healthy young man. Let me tell you something. Men sleep. Women float on the surface, but men go down without fear. How many men have been murdered in their sleep? How many could be? Men sleep in trust; women float."

If this was the reflection of something seen, then it was the most incredible confidence Mary had ever been given — the climax of a career of hunting and waiting. Unfortunately, she did not take it in. She was thinking about Iris and wondering what had gone wrong, why the afternoon had failed, why Iris had gone down the road with a closed face.

Mary was leaving the next weekend, and by next summer the afternoon of betrayal would be forgotten, but Mary daren't wait. It was too risky. Tomorrow she would call on Iris and get the chess game moving again. She could never play fewer than ten games at a time. When she had only nine she thought she had none.

THE CIRCUS

❖

❖

UNLIKE its posters, which had promised a fight between a crocodile and a leopard, the circus, when it came to the village, had no animals save a few starving dogs. At the last minute, in time for the performance, a van that had been held up at Port Bou, on the frontier, arrived with a lion. Among the artistes were a clown, a stout woman who sang and danced, and a girl who climbed a rope and hung limply as if she did not know what to do next. The tourists and the summer people had the best seats in the tent; the villagers, chattering in Catalan, were perched on narrow benches high up and well behind the rest. Their faces in the weak, unsteady light were daubs of ivory paint.

Instead of watching the girl and the rope, Laurie looked back at them. "That would be something to paint," he said to his mother.

"Oh, Laurie, don't go around saying everything is something to paint. No one will ever take you seriously." He understood she might be afraid he would talk too much, like his father. The clicking of fans from the villagers' benches sounded like hail and nearly put him to sleep. The tourists clapped for the girl, who had finally come down to earth, but the Catalans felt she had not done enough, had not risked her life, and they shouted insults. The clown, who came next, rode his bicycle under an avalanche of scorn. Laurie hoped he would get down from the bicycle and walk away, but he carried on as if to applause. It reminded the boy of something he could not put a name to. He shut his eyes and tried to memorize the shapes of shadows, the ivory faces.

143

His mother did not laugh once, not even when the stout woman danced the Twist a few feet away from the lion. They were here at the circus because the money had come. They lived for the post that brought the money, but as soon as it arrived, Ralph, Laurie's father, began seeing how it could be spent. It seemed to worry Ralph when there was money; money was like a strange animal that had to be chased from the house. He would pay a few of the debts in the village, at least in part. He never cleared up a debt. Laurie's mother said it was like stopping a leak with putty. Sometimes less than a week after the money had come the mother had to start asking for credit again, and watching to see if the grocer and the charcoal vendor were writing down the correct amount in their books. After the money had gone, the father would curse the village. He was stranded; he was enslaved by merchants and shopkeepers; he would never get away. But when the money was there and they could have got away, he spent it in the bar, and on strangers, and on outings like the circus.

The mother sat, saying nothing, with a sleeping baby on her lap. Ralph was talking to a stranger. He ignored her, disowning his family, as he often did before people he did not know. He was deep in conversation with a grave elderly man wearing a dark suit. The man had put on a suit to come to the circus on a stifling night, as though he were attending a play or a concert in a large town.

The stranger said seriously, "It must be the last circus of its kind. Look at the clown. He has real bones tied to his ears."

"I'm the last of my kind, too," said Ralph, laughing loudly. He was always friendly, at first.

When they stood up to leave, the elderly man understood that Ralph belonged with these three — the woman, the baby and the boy. Ralph stretched his arms. He was huge.

He looked as if he could crush the stranger with one blow of the hand.

"...married," Laurie heard the stranger say, as they filed out. Ralph was greeting the villagers, kissing the old women and thumping the men on the shoulders. He thought they loved him, because they laughed and smiled; it seemed more important to him to be loved by foreign peasants and fishermen than by his own family. Laurie, who played with the village children, understood that there was a mockery in their acceptance of Ralph, but it was not entirely clear to him and he could not have put it in words. The clock on the village square gave the hour as twenty past one, which meant it was even later. They followed Ralph, headed toward the bar. He had not yet told them to get away from him, to go home and go to bed.

"Of course I'm married," said Ralph pleasantly. "I wouldn't live without a wife. I've had three, but this one is the best. I'd be a sodden, raddled, alcoholic wreck if I hadn't married Chris. Ask her. She'll tell you." The sarcasm was not for the stranger but for the family straggling behind, within earshot. Still charming, he introduced himself, put out his hand. He spoke his own name clearly—Ralph Jennings—and he waited for the other to show he had heard the name before. When there was no recognition, he shrugged. Never mind, he seemed to be telling himself.

"Hare," said the man. He announced it in a sharp way, as if he were really saying "here," to be followed by "sir," as Laurie had been made to speak at his old school, before they came to live in Spain. Ralph strode with his hands in his pockets. The man named Hare walked smartly at his side, keeping up with neat, even steps. Laurie and his mother fell back, and she said, "That's an Army walk,

Laurie. He looks as though he'd always worn proper clothes in a hot climate to set an example, doesn't he?"

"Is that a good thing?" said Laurie, pretty certain that Ralph would have said it was not. He minded being back here with his mother and the baby. He would rather have been with the men.

Ralph sat down at a table in the bar and immediately seemed to be filling the room. Hare stood, waiting for Chris and the children. He held her chair. "I don't know about this modern stuff," he said to Ralph. "I saw some of Francis Bacon's pictures in the Sunday *Times*. To tell you the truth, I wouldn't have given a shilling for the lot."

"Have you ever given a shilling for any painting of any kind?" said Ralph. "If you have, it almost gives you the right to have an opinion."

He sounded violent, but Laurie sensed it was still all right. The proprietor of this bar knew that the money had come. He laughed, and shook hands, and brought a bottle of Fundador and four glasses to their table. He accepted Ralph's invitation to have a glass with them, and he left the bottle there. The mother called after him: Laurie would have a grenadine-and-soda, please. Calling, turning her head, she had drawn Ralph's attention. He sat back and stared, as if he had not noticed her until now. He was sick that Hare had not recognized his name, even though Hare knew about Francis Bacon only because he had seen him in the Sunday *Times*.

"What the bloody hell kind of top are you wearing?" he said to his wife.

She had made a blouse with two cotton scarves. The ends were tied round her neck and under her breasts. Her arms were bare. "It's new," she said, as confidently as if she were sure of praise.

"It is most attractive," said Hare.

"Who do you dress for here, anyway?" said Ralph. "The summer lot? Do you want the beach queers to say 'Darling, you look ravishing'?"

Laurie put his head down on the edge of the table and watched the grenadine curling in soda water like red mist. She never defended herself. It was maddening; it made him want to join the attack. Presently he felt his mother stroking his hair. It was an absent-minded gesture. She was thinking of something else.

"I wish I had married," Laurie heard. "But, you see, seventeen years in the Singapore police...and we had ideals. Fifteen bachelors we were, all in our thirties, and none of us ever had a mistress. You see, it was all an ideal."

"Christ."

"Then I was sorry I hadn't married, but it was too late. I felt stranded. I can't think of another word. It was like being left behind. I knew it was too late. There was a nurse, an Army nurse, but I never dared ask. She would have refused."

Laurie moved his head, and his mother's hand slid away. He sat up, blinking, and was astonished to see the stranger more excited, more talkative even than Ralph.

"It must be hard to feel stranded," said Laurie's mother.

"Yes, we can't imagine that, can we?" said Ralph, looking at her with hate.

"I felt that if a woman came to me she would be giving up something more important than I could replace," said Hare. "How would you feel if someone took your wife away from you?"

"If someone did *what*? Why? Do you want her?"

"Don't," said his wife, and she looked at the other man, but he must have misunderstood her look, for he went on, making it worse: "A woman with a sense of duty."

"She's got that, all right. Would you go with him,

Chris? Let's hear about your sense of duty. Would you go off with our new friend Hare if he asked you?"

"If he asked me to," she said, making a statement to herself. "If he asked me? I don't know."

Ralph put his great hands flat on the table, pushing glasses every way. He said, "Would you consider it? Would you think of going away?"

"If I went, I'd be going away," she said. She sounded reasonable.

"You wouldn't leave the children." Suddenly realizing that of course she would not, he cried, "I wouldn't give them to you! Try taking them. Just try!"

The stranger looked at her with fear and wonder, because she had not said no. He spoke as if out of a dream: "Would you leave? Would you come away if it meant giving up your children?"

"It's hard to say," said the mother. "I might. There's no telling."

"Could you do that?" said Hare, marvelling.

"I've never had to decide."

Laurie said, "I don't feel well."

His mother did not move or speak or feel his forehead.

"The boy's ill," said Ralph. He looked at his wife and said, "Take me home."

Ralph was hurt; he said they had hurt him, all of them. Walking home, he held Laurie's hand, although Laurie was too old for that. Hare had gone down to the beach to see the sun rise. The sky was lightening, as if drawing away. Laurie had sometimes frightened himself with two ideas: his mother might take him away from Ralph (where to?) or else she never would. He had never supposed she could go away alone. She walked in silence, as she always did, but now it was the father and Laurie who lagged behind. She led the way home. Tears rolled

down Ralph's cheeks. He said now that he was hurt
because she had not liked the circus. What about the old
lion who blinked and put out a paw? What about the
clown?

"It was the last circus in the world," he said. "We shall
never see anything like it again."

She had said she might go—at least that she could
consider it—but she was still here. She was here, shifting
the weight of the baby so that she could get the door key
out of her purse and let them into the house.

"It was the last of its kind," said Ralph, who really
seemed to have nothing but this to feel sorry about. "We
shall never see anything like it again."

Laurie, who was watching his mother, squeezed his
hand. "Please stop saying it," he said.

IN TRANSIT

❖

❖

AFTER the Cook's party of twenty-five Japanese tourists had departed for Oslo, only four people were left in the waiting room of the Helsinki Airport—a young French couple named Perrigny, who had not been married long, and an elderly pair who were identifiably American. When they were sure that the young people two benches forward could not understand them, the old people went on with a permanent, flowing quarrel. The man had the habit of reading signs out loud, though perhaps he did it only to madden his wife. He read the signs over the three doors leading out to the field: "'Oslo.' 'Amsterdam.' 'Copenhagen.'...I don't see 'Stockholm.'"

She replied, "What I wonder is what I have been to you all these years."

Philippe Perrigny, who understood English, turned around, pretending he was looking at Finnish pottery in the showcases on their right. He saw that the man was examining timetables and tickets, all the while muttering "Stockholm, Stockholm," while the woman looked away. She had removed her glasses and was wiping her eyes. How did she arrive at that question here, in Helsinki Airport, and how can he answer? It has to be answered in a word: everything/nothing. It was like being in a country church and suddenly hearing the peasant priest put a question no one cares to consider, about guilt or duty or the presence of God, and breathing with relief when he has got past that and on to the prayers.

"In the next world we will choose differently," the man said. "At least I know you will."

The wild thoughts of the younger man were: They are chained for the rest of this life. Too old to change? Only a brute would leave her now? They are walking toward the door marked "Amsterdam," and she limps. That is why they cannot separate; she is an invalid. He has been looking after her for years. They are going through the Amsterdam door, whatever their tickets said. Whichever door they take, they will see the circular lanes of suburbs, and the family car outside each house, and in the back yard a blue pool. All across Northern Europe streets are named after acacia trees, but they may not know that.

Perrigny was on his wedding trip, but also on assignment for his Paris paper, and he assembled the series on Scandinavia in his mind. He had been repeating for four years now an article called "The Silent Cry," and neither his paper nor he himself had become aware that it was repetitious. He began to invent again, in the style of the Paris weeklies: "It was a silent anguished cry torn from the hearts and throats..." No. "It was a silent song, strangled..." "It was a silent passionate hymn to..." This time the beginning would be joined to the blue-eyed puritanical north; it had applied to Breton farmers unable to get a good price for their artichokes, to the Christmas crowd at the Berlin Wall, to Greece violated by tourists, to Negro musicians performing at the Olympia music hall, to miserable Portuguese fishermen smuggled into France and dumped on the labour market, to poets writing under the influence of drugs.

The old man took his wife's hand. She was still turned away, but dry-eyed now, and protected by glasses. To distract her while their tickets were inspected he said rapidly, "Look at the nice restaurant, the attractive restaurant. It is part outside and part inside, see? It is inside *and* outside."

Perrigny's new wife gently withdrew her hand from his and said, "Why did you leave her?"

He had been expecting this, and said, "Because she couldn't concentrate on one person. She was nice to everybody, but she couldn't concentrate enough for a marriage."

"She was unfaithful."

"That too. It came from the same lack of concentration. She had been married before."

"Oh? She was old?"

"She's twenty-seven now. She was afraid of being twenty-seven. She used to quote something from Jane Austen—an English writer," he said as Claire frowned. "Something about a woman that age never being able to hope for anything again. I wonder what she did hope for."

"The first husband left her, too?"

"No, he died. They hadn't been married very long."

"You *did* leave her?" said the girl, for fear of a possible humiliation—for fear of having married a man some other woman had thrown away.

"I certainly did. Without explanations. One Sunday morning I got up and dressed and went away. I came back when she wasn't there and took my things away—my tape recorder, my records. I came back twice for my books. I never saw her again except to talk about the divorce."

"Weren't you unhappy, just walking out that way? You make it sound so easy."

"I don't admire suffering," he said, and realized he was echoing his first wife. Suffering was disgusting to her; the emblem of dirt was someone like Kafka alone in a room distilling blows and horror.

"Nobody admires suffering," said the girl, thinking of aches and cramps. "She had a funny name."

"Yes, terrible. Shirley. She always had to spell it over

the phone. Suzanne Henri Irma Robert Louis Émile Yvonne. It is not pronounced as it is spelled."

"Were you really in love with her?"

"I was the first time I saw her. The mistake was that I married her. The mystery was why I ever married her."

"Was she pretty?"

"She had lovely hair, like all the American girls, but she was always cutting it and making it ugly. She had good legs, but she wore flat shoes. Like all the Americans, she wore her clothes just slightly too long, and with the flat shoes...she never looked dressed. She was blind as a mole and wore dark glasses because she had lost the other ones. When she took her glasses off, sometimes she looked ruthless. But she was worried and impulsive, and thought men had always exploited her."

Claire said, "How do I know you won't leave me?" but he could tell from her tone she did not expect an answer to that.

Their flight was called. They moved out under "Copenhagen," carrying their cameras and raincoats. He was glad this first part of the journey was over. He and Claire were together the whole twenty-four hours. She was good if he said he was working, but puzzled and offended if he read. Attending to her, he made mistakes. In Helsinki he had gone with her to buy clothes. Under racks of dresses he saw her legs and bare feet. She came out, smiling, holding in front of herself a bright dress covered with suns. "You can't wear it in Paris," he said, and he saw her face change, as if he had darkened some idea she'd had of what she might be. In a park, yesterday, beside a tall spray of water, he found himself staring at another girl, who sat feeding squirrels. He admired the back of her neck, the soft parting of her hair, her brown shoulder and arm. Idleness of this kind never happened in what he chose to think of as real life—as if love and travel were opposed to living, were a dream. He drew closer to his new wife, this blond summer child, thinking of the winter honeymoon with his first wife. He had read her hand to distract her from the cold and rain, holding the leaf-palm, tracing the extremely shallow head line (no judgment, he informed her) and the choppy life—an American life, he had said, folding the leaf. He paid attention to Claire, because he had admired another girl and had remembered something happy with his first wife, all in a minute. How would Claire like to help him work, he said. Together they saw how much things cost in shop windows, and she wrote down for him how much they paid for a meal of fried fish and temperance beer. Every day had to be filled as never at home. A gap of two hours in a strange town, in transit, was like being shut up in a stalled lift with nothing to read.

Claire would have given anything to be the girl in the park, to have that neck and that hair *and* stand off and see it, all at once. She saw the homage he paid the small ears, the lobes pasted. She had her revenge in the harbour, later, when a large group of tourists mistook her for someone famous—for an actress, she supposed. She had been told she looked like Catherine Deneuve. They held out cards and papers and she signed her new name, "Claire Perrigny," "Claire Perrigny," over and over, looking back at him with happy triumphant eyes. Everything flew and shrieked around them—the sea-gulls, the wind, the strangers calling in an unknown language something she took to mean "Your name, your name!"

"They think I am famous!" she called, through her thick flying hair. She smiled and grinned, in conspiracy, because she was not famous at all, only a pretty girl who had been married eight days. Her tongue was dark with the blueberries she had eaten in the market—until Philippe had told her, she hadn't known what blueberries were. She smiled her stained smile, and tried to catch her soaring skirt between her knees. Compassion, pride, tenderness, jealousy and acute sick misery were what he felt in turn. He saw how his first wife had looked before he had ever known her, when she was young and in love.

THE STATUES
TAKEN DOWN

❖

❖

CRAWLEY turned his two younger children loose day after day in the Palais-Royal gardens, because he thought it would keep them amused, but they were not brought up to spend a whole afternoon sitting on iron chairs. They had not, as Crawley imagined children must have, any kind of secret language or code. It was convenient for him to imagine they were close and inviolate and that he, as an adult, was excluded, but all Hal and Dorothy had in common was their colouring, which was fair, and houses lived in—they lived with their grandmother in Dutchess County, or in New York City with their mother when she could have them—and journeys shared, and the American tongue. Their accent made them sound alien, for Crawley's older children, by another wife, were English, like their father.

"The first time I met your mother," said Crawley, as if speaking to children who had no connection with that particular person, "I was flat on my back in the American Hospital and she very efficiently and almost patiently— you know how nurses are always in a hurry—drew quite a lot of blood from my arm, perhaps to measure the degree of alcohol. I had been brought in after a fistfight. She looked like the Holbein portrait of Lady Parker, with that sweet mouth and almost lashless blue eyes, and the hair parted in the centre, and a flat coif around the back of the head, and I had not yet heard her speak. I said, 'I love you, and will you marry me?' She smiled and went away, and the next day she came again, and I said, 'My name is George Crawley, I love you, will you marry me?'

She smiled, and measured the blood she had taken against the light, but still did not speak. I said, 'I am divorced, but even if you are a Catholic there is no impediment, for I was never married in church.' She said then, in a soft voice, 'I am almost engaged to the doctor I've been working with in Malaya.' 'Is he still in the East?' said I. 'No,' she said, 'I am talking about the American doctor *in Malaya*.' And what do you think she was saying?"

He looked from one face to the other and was looking not at his own children but at images of Victorian children in repose, between reprimands, safely over whatever they had been deprived of that morning in the way of food or comfort and considering the safest way of avoiding an unknown offence. They were Victorian in expression, in watchful calm. The girl's rather thin blond hair was held by a red band. The boy wore a shirt with a big sign of the zodiac printed on it. "What she was saying," Crawley rushed on, aware now that he was telling these children about their mother, "was 'the doctor in my lab.'" He hurried the end, though it was a story that had made many other people laugh. The children thought it was a reasonable mistake for George to have made, for he was slightly hard of hearing.

Crawley spoke a peculiar sort of English, full of idioms translated literally from French—he had lived in France such a long time. He said of a lodger now staying in his flat, "I took him on as a favour to a friend. Actually, I don't like his head," meaning "There is something about him I dislike." He did not know how funny he sounded. He had a nose broken like a boxer's, and a head of thick, curly grey hair. He did not look like their last memory of him, which was three years old, or their mother's description, which was not physical but only that he was a poet. He did not resemble his pictures. He seemed heavier, softer. He said he hoped the lodger would find another place to stay. He said this quite loudly, but without petulance. He might go on saying it the whole summer long. As for the lodger, he closed doors silently and laid the telephone back on its cradle as if it might explode. The trace of his presence was humble, such as a nylon shirt dripping at the kitchen window, or a hairbrush he kept (it seemed its permanent abode) on the edge of the tub. This brush, backed by some transparent and thumb-printed plastic material, its jagged and gleaming bristles faintly coated with oil and a web of fine hair, told Dorothy, the elder of the children, that George suffered from a kind of blindness. He saw only what he wanted to; otherwise, he would surely have told the lodger to keep his personal stuff in a drawer. The children believed that the lodger did not like them. This was of no consequence. They were not dependent on their charm, and understood claims of a practical nature, outside the domain of love. The lodger was only a pale eye, a hostile and melancholy nose glimpsed when he opened his door an inch or two—it sometimes happened that he was wanted on the telephone. He seemed a failed adult, therefore a kind of weed. Had he been where nature meant him to be, growing in plant form, by a dusty path, and not here, where he was not desired and not expected—had he been, say, a dandelion clock, the girl's summer skirt could have brushed off his head and she would never have noticed the harm.

Dorothy could remember three summers in Paris, Hal only two. This year, so as to have room for them, their father had sublet a sunless, high-ceilinged place that smelled like a pet shop. The lodger, in some complicated way, had come with the flat, which, in turn, was the property of a girl named Natasha. At first it was cold—so cold that Dorothy wore a sweater under a raincoat and Hal walked with his head pulled down, as if the act of shortening his neck would keep him warm. The blooming of the city, of the chestnut trees in particular, was four to six weeks late. They saw the legendary trees, round as sponges, covered with little green lettuce leaves. A frost, said Hal, would finish them off. Then all at once it was a true summer, with a wilderness of leaves, and that was something Dorothy remembered. She confused plane and linden and chestnut, though one of them had flowers, for she did not know trees at home, except for birches and elms. Dust blew up in their faces when they entered the closed park of the Palais-Royal. It was smaller than the space retained in their minds. It would continue to shrink; perhaps they would come back grown and find it the size of a drying sheet. A red chestnut tree, as they approached it, became pink; from underneath, the flowers were pink as floss. They trod on fallen petals, which from a distance were again red. Venturing out and farther, they saw great flapping flags on high, cold, imposing standards.

"Those are for some Negro king," said Dorothy, the elder, the informed. "Father told me."

"Which king?" said the boy, not wishing to say he had never seen one. He invented eyes, robes, a coronet and sticking-out ears.

"It means an important visitor," said Dorothy. "When they have an important visitor here, they call him a Negro king." She smoothed her hair as she explained, developing conscious, feminine conceit. Had she been older, she would have asked now for a cigarette and held it just so for the flame. She did not know whether she ought to say "Father told me" or "George" or something more foreign-sounding. "George" thought he was the centre of the universe and that the planets, highly polished and lighted from within, circled round him, chanting his praises. But "your father" was also generous and impulsive and unreliable and famous—this last they had only recently been told, by their mother. If true, then why the lodger? Why no cleaning woman, and why furniture sagging or cigarette-burned or mended with glue? Some piece of information about him had been overlooked or misunderstood. Quite often they were handed information they could not use and did not understand. For example, their grandmother kept geraniums in her kitchen in large Crisco tins, and said it was because the depression had marked her.

In the Palais-Royal, Hal played soccer with an unknown boy until a guard put a stop to it. He bought ice cream on a stick, an egg puzzle of polished wood that came apart and could not be put together, comic books he could not enjoy because they were in French, and a bracelet of make-believe jade for his mother. And then he kicked Dorothy's chair and said, "What'll we do?" Dorothy read a green-backed pornographic novel she had found on the bathroom window sill. It was smug and precise, and full of what she took to be the wrong information. She knew and had known for some years that you do not have babies by kissing, but the private anarchy here described could not be truthful, either. When she saw couples kissing, perfectly still, pressed together under the late-blooming trees, she reverted to an earlier, childish belief, and thought they were in danger.

The Palais-Royal became too small; she moved with Hal to the Tuileries, and there, for the first time, she read her father's poems. One of them told how a swallow in a narrow street, skimming too low, migrating, was caught in a net. Crawley, when he saw Dorothy carrying the book, and opened it to that page, was heedless or unknowing enough to say, "That was your mother." If Dorothy had seen swallows, she had not recognized them; she could not imagine a street so narrow that a net would reach across it, or a bird too clumsy to fly up and away. A pigeon, perhaps, if it had been wounded first. Even the pigeons— she saw many of them here—could scatter like gunfire. Her mother was not a bird that waddled or went off in some foolish direction. If she had been a bird, she would have walked on long legs, though she was not like a picture of a stork, or bright as a postcard flamingo. The pigeons' neck feathers were iridescent, their square tail feathers like lopped-off fans....

Hal said, "What'll we do, Dottie? Are we just going to hang around here?" If you sat on an iron chair, you had to pay for it. She found a cinema for him, a place that showed nothing but horror movies. The sign outside said "Festival du Vampire" and also that no one under sixteen would be admitted, but this rule did not appear to be enforced. She abandoned him there; he was to meet her later in the park. Hours later she was shocked—drawn awake, in a sense—by a darkening across the sky, as if black wool were being combed out in great streaks. It coincided with the rushing movement she had already observed at a certain hour, when people fled home. They did not get up and go quietly, they ran away. She looked at lovers again, and then at entwined statues. (Hal was seeing the vampire festival the third time through, eating chocolate in the dark to give him energy so that he could bear his emotions.) The intimation of danger here, in the park, the sudden rush of the clouds, made her think sentimentally of her father, alone and possibly lonely. The wind, rising, was heavy and hot. She was fed up with Hal, with his weight as a brother. He would have to find his own way home.

Closing her book, she saw that the lovers and the children around her had been replaced by idle men, and that she was watched from benches and chairs and from behind trees. Her spine was stiff from the iron chair. The lovers, the children, the mothers, the grandmothers had disappeared, leaving the entwined and emotional statues and these silent men. It was as though animals had crept out of their cages and were afraid to do more than stare. It was not yet night. With theatrical precision, thunder shuddered in the air. She got up and walked away, the last girl in the park. Hal, in communion with American vampires, was certainly safe. He might be on his way home, or here, hoping to find her.

Nothing she wanted to know, either about her sudden fear or her sudden cruelty—the way she wanted to be rid of Hal—had been explained in her father's poems. The sound of the lodger stealthily closing doors, the dwindling thunder, the whisper of traffic as she approached the rue de Rivoli—these indications that she could at least *hear*—were no help to her; they were fugitive, suggestive sounds, like the clues to her father's past. They were as close, and as evocative, and as general as his early life with their mother, or his life with someone else. Other people moved behind walls of gossip. Dorothy could look at pictures; she could read George's diaries, for he had let them be printed. It was hard to believe he had ever had a secret. He told of lying in bed with a sister-in-law while his wife lay with a newly born son in a nursing home not far away. Dorothy could have questioned anyone, even the lodger; George would never have thought it a betrayal. He lied only sometimes, suiting a fancy.

Because she knew that Hal trusted her and that she had left the park on a pretext of fear—no, perhaps she had been frightened, but when she paused, deciding this, it was too late to go back—she seemed to herself inferior and unworthy of the poet's past. He was said to have been courageous. The women he had known had been brave too, though some had been other things—beautiful, multilingual, insane, alcoholic, notorious, discussed. All but her own mother, the one he had called Lady Someone in a picture, and a swallow in a poem. She had been the most useful wife, because she had nursed him. But when George talked about women he said, "That was a real woman," as though anyone else was only pretending. He said "Natasha," or "Portia," or "Felicia"—real women had names that ended in "a." The names evoked, for his daughter, their large breasts and abundant hair, their repeated pregnancies and their chain-smoking. They had been photographed when the camera was askew or the light bleak, when their hair was lank after rain, when their babies half slipped off their corduroy laps like parcels on a bus. She imagined them not as they had sat for false cameras but as they must have been in life. She was from a thinner generation, a generation of stick figures. Figures from his time seemed twice the size of life. "Is it true," her father asked, as if she should know, "that they are taking down the statues in the Tuileries and replacing them with Maillols?" She did not know, and he did not bestir himself to see. "They were wild and romantic," he said, "and the Maillols are going to look damned silly with pigeons on their heads."

The children met Natasha close to the end of their stay. Her arms were thin as a starved child's. Her black sweater and checked skirt, her black stockings and pixie shoes made her seem a child from an institution. She had invented her own uniform. She removed the cotton scarf that protected her from the driving August rain, and a great puff of dyed hair rose like a fan. Pencilled brows arched, clownlike, on a high, bald brow. She had somehow found a puddle to walk in—around her shoes water collected. Elf-sized lakes were created, and then, because of the inclination of the ancient floor, a pair of rivers. She had not come to stay but only to visit. The lodger had departed under circumstances that had been kept from Hal until now, and from Dorothy until yesterday: he had shot himself in the courtyard of the Palais de Justice and, still alive, had been taken to a hospital.

"Two forces hung over him for most of his childhood," said Natasha.

"His mother and father, like everyone," said George.

"No, George. Hitler and Stalin." Then she said, staring, "Oh, these are the *nurse's* children," and George stared, too, as if children, unless legends, with warm, wild and legendary mothers, confounded him. He lit his pipe with watery old-man sounds.

"Don't exaggerate," he said to Natasha. "Don't exaggerate." This was new, this repeating everything as if other people were slightly deaf. Natasha sat in her chair and seemed to be cowering. He had said of her, to Dorothy, "She is a remarkable woman, with considerable charm. She has a rackety sort of life." The story had been notorious once: George had persuaded Natasha to elope from Moscow, and then he had left her and gone to live with the Austrian translator of his poems. He blurred the story in the telling, having perhaps forgotten much of it. Dorothy knew one thing—the swallow had rushed away from him. That put her outside the legend and outside his generation, in a way. When he talked of his generation, he said it was well-tempered, and Dorothy thought, Kind, he means—they were kind. He confused the living and the dead, or seemed to. When Dorothy started saying "generation," he stopped her and said, "You have none. We were a well-tempered crowd."

Speaking of the lodger, Natasha said, "He knows he is dying. He knows I have called his father in Moscow. He knows his father cannot get a visa. Well, this has been the worst day of my life. I feel close to death."

"You aren't," said George. "He is."

"He cannot lift his head from the pillow. If you would help me, George, if you would accept some of the responsibility."

"Accept!" cried the man, and with a blunt gesture took in the boy and the girl. "I ask for it, I *assume* it, when it is mine. *You* brought him out of Russia."

"Well, the only thing to be done...I suppose I should take him some soap."

"Yes, yes, take him some soap," said George, but without vehemence now. He looked at Dorothy as if he had her between himself and death in a public hospital. He mentioned the things his loyal daughter would bring him when the time came: "Soap, a razor, rubbing alcohol and a toothbrush."

"That is what I decided," said Natasha. "That was what I had decided before I came to see you. I thought it was the only thing to do—take him some soap."

"You shouldn't forget this," said the children's father. "It is more important than you think." Dorothy, playing at being mistress of the house, emptied Natasha's ashtray. Hal stolidly tried to put together the egg puzzle he had bought in the early days, at the Palais-Royal. He had all the pieces, nothing was missing, but still could not make it whole. Dorothy pulled everything she knew apart and started from the begnning. My mother looked like Lady Something in a Holbein. George was a swallow. My mother was the net.

QUESTIONS
AND ANSWERS

❖

RUMANIANS notoriously are marked by delusions of eminence and persecution, and Madame Gisèle does not encourage them among her clientele. She never can tell when they are trying to acquire information, or present some grievance that were better taken to a doctor or the police. Like all expatriates in Paris, they are concerned with the reactions of total strangers. She is expected to find in the cards the functionary who sneered, the flunky who behaved like a jailer, the man who, for no reason, stared too long at the plates of the car. Madame Gisèle prefers her settled clients—the married women who sit down to say, "When is my husband going to die?" and "What about the man who smiles at me every morning on the bus?" She can find him easily: There he is—the jack of hearts. One of the queens is not far away, along with the seven of diamonds turned upside down. Forget about him. He is supporting his mother and has already deserted a wife.

Amalia Moraru has been visiting Madame Gisèle for two years now. She has been so often, and her curiosity is so flickering and imprecise, that Madame Gisèle charges her for time, like a garage. Amalia asks questions about her friend Marie.

"Marie used to be so pretty," Amalia begins, taking no notice of Madame Gisèle's greeting, which is "You again!" "Thirty years ago we used to say she looked French. That was a compliment in Bucharest. You know, we are a Latin race in that part of the country...."

Madame Gisèle, who is also Rumanian but from one of

the peripheral provinces, replies, "Who cares?" She and Amalia both speak their language badly. Amalia was educated in French, which was the fashion for Bucharest girls of her background thirty years ago, while the fortune-teller is at home in a Slavic-sounding dialect.

"Marie must be very ill now," Amalia says cautiously, "to have stopped looking so French. Last night in the Place du Marché St-Honoré, people were staring at her. She smiles at anyone. My husband thinks she has lost her mind. Her legs are swollen. What do you see? Heart trouble? Circulation?"

"Overwork. What makes you think *you* look French?"

A long glance in the magic hand mirror, lying face upward on the table, assures Amalia that if she does not seem French it is entirely to her credit. Her collar is pressed, her hair is coiled and railed in by pins. She tries something else: "I have Marie's new X-rays—the ones she's had taken for the Americans."

"I've already told you, I am not a doctor."

"You could look at them. You can tell so much from just a snapshot sometimes."

"I can in a normal consultation. You brought me a picture once. You said, 'This is my old friend in Bucharest. Do you see a journey for her?' 'Everyone travels,' I told you. But I did look, and I did see a journey...."

"You even saw the broken light bulbs in the train, and the unswept floors," says Amalia, encouraging her.

"I know what Rumanian trains have been like since the war. Your friend came to Paris. What more did you want?"

"Why hasn't she said anything about the money certain people owe her? What does Marie think about certain people when she is alone?"

Madame Gisèle will not look in the hand mirror, or the ball, she will not burn candles to collect the wax, because

Amalia pays a low rate for her time. She does keep one hand on the cards, in case a question should be asked she feels she can answer. The seven of hearts would indicate the trend of Marie's most secret thoughts, but Madame Gisèle cannot find it. When she does, nothing around it makes sense.

"Succès légers en amour," announces Madame Gisèle, who is accustomed to making such statements in French.

"Jesus Maria. We are talking about an old woman. Try again."

"Cadeau agréable."

"She buys presents, but I've already told you that. What is she thinking *this minute?*"

"Cut the cards yourself. Left hand.... *Naissance,"* says Madame Gisèle, examining the result. "Monday is a bad day. Go home and come back on a Friday."

Amalia supposes that on this April day Marie is collecting more information about herself for the Americans. Marie hopes to emigrate before long. From time to time she receives a letter requesting a new piece of evidence for her file. She is enjoying April, or pretends to. She waddles to the flower market when she can, and has already brought Amalia the first yellow daffodils of the year. 'Make a wish," says Marie. Her teeth are like leaves in winter now. Does she really think the Americans will let her into the country with that ruined smile? "The first daffodils—wish on them, Amalia. Wish for something." Marie is always wishing. Amalia could understand it in a young person, but at Marie's age what is it all about?

This is not a pleasant April. Some mornings the air is so white and still you might expect a fall of snow, and at night the sky expands, as it does in December.

"Marie is lucky," Amalia remarks, to Madame Gisèle. "She came here when there was plenty of work, and nobody thinks of saying 'refugee' anymore. She has her own passport. Dino and I have never had one. She doesn't know how things were for us fifteen, sixteen years ago. We gave a pearl ring for one CARE parcel, but it had been sold three times and there was nothing in it except rancid butter and oatmeal."

Madame Gisèle is trying again for the seven of hearts. Amalia feels a draft and tugs the collar of her coat around her neck. All over Paris the heating has been turned off too soon. Marie must suffer with the cold. She is a *corsetière,* and kneels to fat women all day. Her legs, her knees, her wrists, her fingers are bloated—she looks like a carving in stone.

"Rendez-vous la nuit," says Madame Gisèle. "Look, I am sick of your friend Marie. Either she knows and is laughing at us or it is you bringing low-class spirits in the room."

"Not laughing—wishing."

On an April evening Marie, in slow march time, approaches her house and sixth-floor room in the Place du Marché St-Honoré. Her legs are thick as boots. Crossing the street she suddenly stands still and begins to watch the sky. You would think her mind was drifting if you could see her, choosing to block traffic at the worst moment of the day, staring at the new moon and the planet Venus. She is making a wish. Amalia, who lives on the same square, has seen her doing it. Marie stares as if the sky were a reflecting sheet; perhaps what Marie sees against blue Venus is the streaky moment of cars behind her, and the shadow of her own head.

Peering into Madame Gisèle's magic hand mirror again to see what *she* can see, Amalia does not recognize her own face. Two years ago, when she knew that Marie would be coming to Paris, Amalia dyed her greying hair. Later, she saw her reflection in the glass covering an old

176

photograph of Marie (the photograph taken to Madame Gisèle for mystical guesswork) and she saw two faces and believed them to be both her own. What am I now, she wondered. I am the one I left and the other one I became. Marie is still herself....Now Amalia knows she was mistaken; Marie is also two. When Marie did arrive in Paris, when she got down from the train that terrifying morning and lumbered toward them, out of the past, holding out her arms, Dino and Amalia would never have known her if Marie had not cried out their names. They had been waiting all night for the past, and they were embraced by a ridiculous stranger who had no one to love but them. Dino pushed out his lips in the Eastern grimace of triumph and contempt, but close to his frightened heart, with his work permit and residence permit and proof of existence and assurance of identity and evidence of domicile, he carried—still carries—a folded piece of paper covered with figures in red ink. It is a statement of account for Marie, if ever she should ask for it. It will show how little Dino received for the rings and gold pieces she gave Amalia when Dino and Amalia left Bucharest sixteen years ago. "Send for me later," Marie had said, and they kissed on the promise. Dino has a round face, blond hair, small uptilted blue eyes and a nose like a cork on a bottle, but of course he is pure Rumanian—a Latin, that is. There is not a drop of foreign blood in any of them: no Greek, no Turkish, no Magyar, no Slav, no Teuton, no Serb. He is represented in the cards by the king of clubs, a dark card, but Amalia prefers it to diamonds. Diamonds mean "stranger."

Madame Gisèle turns the hand mirror face down, because when Amalia looks in it she is getting more than her money's worth.

"Oh, why did Marie ever come here?" Amalia says. In Bucharest they would have given her a pension, in time.

177

They might have sent her to a rest home on the Black Sea. Who will look after her during the long, last illness every *émigré* dreads? Amalia wonders, "What if Marie is insane?"

With the word "insane" she is trying to describe Marie's wishing, her belief that the planets can hear. Amalia is an old expatriate; she knows how to breathe under water. Marie is too old to learn. She belongs to irrecoverable time—that has been the trouble from the beginning. She came to Paris nearly two years ago, and has been wishing for something ever since.

This is a common story. Madame Gisèle's clients are forever worried about lunacy in friends and loved ones. With her left hand she cuts the deck and peers at the queen of diamonds—the stranger, the mortal enemy, the gossip and poisoner of the mind. Surely not Marie?

"Your friend is not insane," says Madame Gisèle abruptly. "She found work without your help. She has found a room to live in."

"Yes, by talking to a Rumanian on the street! What Rumanian? What do we know about him? She talks to anybody. Why did she leave certain people who made a home for her even when they had no room, and even bought her a bed? She found work, yes, but she spends like a fool. Why does she bring certain people the first strawberries of the season? They haven't asked for anything. They can live on soup and apples. Marie is old and sick and silly. She says, 'Look, Amalia, look at the new moon.' What do you know about Marie? You don't know anything."

"Why do you come, if you don't want to hear what I say?" shouts Madame Gisèle, in her village dialect. "Your brain is mildewed, your husband murdered his mother, your friend is a whore!"

These are standard insults and no more offensive than a sneeze. *"Parlons français,"* says Amalia, folding her hands on Marie's X-rays. She will furnish proof of

Marie's dementia, if she can—it seems an obligation suddenly.

"I am the last to deny that Marie was a whore," she begins. "She was kept by a married man. When Dino and I were engaged and I brought him to her flat for the first time, she answered the door dressed in her underwear. But remember that in Bucharest we are a Latin race, and in the old days it was not uncommon for a respectable man to choose an apartment, select the furniture and put a woman in it. After this man's wife died, he would have married Marie, but it was too late. He was too ill. Marie nursed this man when he was dying. She could have left with Dino and me but she stayed."

"It was easier for two to come out then than three," says Madame Gisèle, to whom this is not a complete story. "Certain people may have encouraged her to stay behind."

"If everyone left, what would become of the country?" says Amalia, which is what every old *émigré* has to say about new arrivals. "Listen to me. I think Marie is insane."

One day, soon after Marie had come to Paris, before she had found work in a shop by talking to a Rumanian on the street, Amalia walked with her in the gardens of the Champs-Élysées. It was by no means a promenade; Amalia was on one of the worried errands that make up her day—this time, going to the snack bar where the cook, who is from Bucharest, saves stale bread for people who no longer need it. Once you have needed this bread, you cannot think of its going to anyone else. Marie walked too slowly—her legs hurt her, and she was admiring the avenue. Amalia left her under a chestnut tree. If the tree had opened and encased Marie, Amalia would have thought, God is just, for Marie was a danger, and her presence might pull Amalia and Dino back and down to trouble with the police, which is to say the floor of the sea.

"Listen, Marie," began Amalia to herself, having disposed of Marie on a bench. "We never sent for you because we never were ready. You've seen the hole we live in? We bought it with your rings. We sleep in a cupboard—it has no windows. That piece of cotton hanging is a door. We call this a dining room because it has a table and three chairs—we bought the third chair when we knew you were coming. There is your new bed, between the chair and the curtain. Dino will curse you every time he stumbles against it. The trees of Paris? The flower stalls? We have the biggest garage of Paris in the middle of our square. The square should be called Place du Garage St-Honoré now. I want to tell you also that most of the things you gave me were worth nothing. Only diamonds matter, and the best were stolen when we were coming through Bulgaria and Greece. When we first came to live here, where the garage stands now there were baskets of fruit and flowers."

Returning with her newspaper parcel of stale bread, Amalia looks for Marie. Marie has vanished. Amalia understands that some confused wishing of her own, some abracadabra pronounced without knowing its powers, has caused her old friend to disintegrate. She, Amalia, will be questioned about it.

Marie is not far away. She has left the bench and is sitting on the ground. Pigeons cluster around her—they go to anyone. Her eyes are globed with tears. The tears are suspended, waiting, and every line of her body seems hurt and waiting for greater pain. Whatever has hurt her is nothing to what is to come. Amalia rushes forward, calling. Marie is not crying at all. She holds out a chestnut. "Look," she says.

"Where did it come from?" cries Amalia wildly, as if she has forgotten where she is.

Marie gets to her feet like a great cow. "It was still in its case; it must be left over from last year."

"They turn dark and ugly in a minute," says Amalia, and she throws it away.

As proof of madness this is fairly thin, except for the part about sitting on the ground. Amalia, remembering that she is paying for time, now takes the tack that Madame Gisèle is concealing what she knows. "It is up to you to convince me," she says. *"Will Marie go to America?"*

"Everyone travels," says Madame Gisèle.

Well, that is true. The American consulate is full of ordinary tourists who can pay their passage and will see, they hope, Indian ceremonial dances. Amalia is told that scholars are admitted to the great universities for a year, two years, with nothing required, not even a knowledge of English. Who will want Marie, who actually does speak a little English but has nonsensical legs, no relations and thinks she can sell corsets in a store? Marie filled out the forms they gave her months ago, and received a letter saying, "You are not legible."

"How funny," said the girl in the consulate when Marie and Amalia returned with the letter. "They mean eligible."

"What does it mean?" said Marie.

"It is a mistake, but it means you can't go to the United States. Not as your situation is now."

"If it is a mistake—"

"One word is a mistake."

"Then the whole letter might be wrong."

To Amalia, standing beside her, Marie seems unable to support something just then—perhaps the weight of her own clothes. Amalia reviews her friend's errors—her broken English, her plucked eyebrows, her flat feet in glossy shoes, the fact that she stayed in Rumania when it was time to leave and left when it was better to stay. "Will my clothes be all right for there?" says Marie, because Amalia is staring.

"You may not be going. Didn't you hear the young lady?"

"This isn't the last word, or the last letter. You will see." Marie is confident—she shows her broken teeth.

Madame Gisèle is interested though she has heard this before. She cuts the deck and says, "Here it is—*réception d'une missive peu comprehensible.*"

"Pff—fourteen months ago that was," says Amalia. "Then they wrote and asked for centimetre-by-centimetre enlargements of the pictures of her lungs. You haven't told me why Marie left the friends who had bought her a bed."

"Because she found a room by talking to another Rumanian on the street."

"That is true. But she had the room for days, weeks even, before she decided to leave."

"Something must have made her decide," says Madame Gisèle. "No one can say I am not trying, but your questions are not clear. I am expecting another client, and I have to take the dog out."

"There must be another reason. Look again."

Every evening when she came home from work, Marie helped Amalia chop the vegetables for the evening soup. They sat face to face across a thick board on which were the washed leeks, the potatoes, the onions and the parsley. Amalia wondered if she and Marie looked the same, with their hands misshapen and twisted and the false meekness of their bent heads. Living had bent them, Amalia would begin to say, and emigration, and being women, and oh, she supposed, the war. "At least you didn't marry a peasant," Amalia said once. "At least I know what class I am from. My ancestors could read and write from the time of Julius Caesar, and my grandfather owned his own house." Marie said nothing. "If only we had been men," said Amalia, "or had any amount of money, or lived on a different continent..." She looked up, dreaming, the knife in abeyance.

Sometimes Amalia spoke of Dino. Sometimes she giggled as if she and Marie were still Bucharest girls, convent-trained, French-prattling, with sleek Turkish hair, Greek noses, long amber eyes and not a drop of foreign blood. "Your apartment, Marie?" It was white and gold, Amalia remembered, and there was a row of books that turned out to be not Balzac at all but a concealed bar. There was an original pastel drawing of a naked girl on a diving board, and a musical powder box that played "Valentine." "After I married Dino, we came back sometimes and sat on the white chairs and watched your friends dancing—do you remember, Marie?—and we waited until they had gone, and you would lend us a little money—we always paid it back—and you gave me a fox scarf, and a pin that showed a sleeping fawn, and a hat made of sequins, and perfume from France—Shalimar. I kept the empty bottle. Your life was French...." It has always seemed that the old flat furnished by Marie's dead friend is the real Paris, and the row of Balzac that turns into a bar is the truth about France. "Dino was apprenticed to a glovemaker at the beginning," Amalia said, "and his hands had a queer smell, something to do with the leather, and he never dared ask the girls to dance." Marie went on chopping leeks, holding the knife by the handle and blade in both swollen hands. Amalia said, "He's afraid of you, Marie, because you remember all that. He was always mean and stingy, and he hasn't changed. Remember the first present he ever gave me?"

"A gold locket," said Marie gently.

"Gold? Don't make me laugh. I put it around my neck and said, 'I'll never take it off,' and he said, 'You had better sometimes because the yellow will wear off.'"

She laughed, laughing into the past as if she were no longer afraid of it. "He hasn't changed. I thought of leaving him. Yes, I was going to write to you and say, 'I am leaving him now.' But by then we had so many years of worry behind us, and everywhere I looked that worry was like a big stone in the road."

Marie nodded, as if she knew. She never said much, never confided. Amalia snatched away the last of the vegetables and said, "Let me finish. You are so slow," and then Dino came in and slapped the table with the flat of his hand, so as to send the women flying apart, one to put the soup on the stove and the other to go out and buy the evening paper, which he had forgotten. It happens every night for a year, it can happen all your life, Amalia was thinking, and suddenly you have all those years like a stone. But Marie once sat quietly and said, "Listen, Dino" so carefully that he did seem to hear. "I am not your slave. Perhaps I will be a slave one day, but I don't want to learn the habit of slavery. I am well and strong, and my whole life is before me, and I am working, and I have a room. Yes, I am going to live alone now. Oh, not far away, but somewhere else."

"Who wants you?" Dino shouted, but he was in a cold sweat because of all Marie knew, and because she had never asked about the rings she gave them. Amalia was thinking, She is too ill to live alone. What if she dies? And the rings—she has said nothing about the rings. Why is she leaving me?

She looked around to see what they had done to Marie, but there was no hint of cruelty or want of gratitude in the room. Marie would never guess that Amalia had been to Madame Gisèle, saying, "How do you kill it—the buoyancy, the credulity, the blindness to everything harsh?"

"Marie," Amalia would like to say, "will you admit that working and getting older and dying matter, and can't be countered by the first hyacinth of the year?" But Marie went on packing. Amalia consoled herself: Marie's mind had slipped. She was mad.

Marie straightened up from her packing and smiled. "Three people can't live together. You and Dino will be better alone."

"No, don't leave us alone together," Amalia cried. There must have been some confusion in the room at that moment, because nobody heard.

Last autumn one serious thing happened to Marie—she was in trouble with the police. She says that at the Préfecture—the place every *émigré* is afraid of—they shut her in a room one whole day. Had she been working without a premit? Did she change her address without reporting it? Could her passport be a forgery? Marie only says, "A policeman was rude to me, and I told him never to do it again." Released in the evening, having been jeered at, sequestered, certainly insulted, she crossed the street and began to admire the flower market. She bought a bunch of ragged pink asters and spent the last money she had in her pocket (it seems that at the Préfecture she was made to pay a large fine) on coffee and cakes. She can describe every minute of her adventures after she left the Préfecture: how she bought the asters, with Amalia in mind, how she sat down at a white marble table in a tearoom, and the smoking coffee she admired in the white china cup, and the colour the coffee was when the milk was poured in, and how good it was, how hot. She shares, in the telling, a *baba au rhum*. You can see the fork pressing on the very last crumb, and the paper-lace *napperon* on the plate. Now she chooses to walk along the

Seine, between the ugly evening traffic and the stone parapet above the quay. She is walking miles the wrong way. She crosses a bridge she likes the look of, then another, and sees a clock. It is half past six. From the left of the wooden footbridge that joins the Île Saint-Louis and the Île de la Cité, she looks back and falls in love with the sight of Notre Dame; the scanty autumn foliage beneath it is bright gold. Everything is gold but the sky, which is mauve, and contains a new moon. She has spent all her money, and cannot wish on the new moon without a coin in her hand. She stops a passerby by touching him on the arm. Stiff with outrage, he refuses to let her hold even a one-centime piece so that she can wish. She has to wish on the moon without a coin, holding a second-class métro ticket instead—all that her pocket now contains. She turns the ticket over as if it were silver, and wishes for something with all her heart.

Marie tells Dino and Amalia about it. It can only irritate them, but she hasn't sense enough to keep it to herself. They are concerned about the police: "What happened? What did they say?"

"Nothing," says Marie. "They gave me a card. I can stay in France another year."

"Not a year; three months," says Dino angrily. "It is three months and three months and three months..." She shows the card to him. It is the red card—she may stay a year. That is the beginning. Probably she can stay forever.

"They have made a mistake," says Dino.

The police never make a mistake. She is an elderly refugee with a chronic illness and no money, and she has broken some rule and even lectured a policeman, they have shut her up a whole day, and yet they have given her this. Dino returns the card—he holds it as if it were crystal.

"If I were afraid of policemen," says Marie, casually

putting the object in her purse, "I wouldn't have left Rumania with a passport, and I wouldn't be here with you now."

They are gagged with shame at what they suspect about each other's thoughts. Before she came, each of them hoped she would be arrested at some frontier and taken off the train. They never wanted her.

Amalia, from this moment, considers Marie a witch. What does she say to herself when she turns a métro ticket over, staring at the new moon? Wishes have no power to correct the past—even credulous Marie must know it. Madame Gisèle says most women ask about their husbands, or other men. When Amalia goes to Madame Gisèle, it is to ask about Marie.

"I think I know your secret," Madame Gisèle said once.

Amalia's heart stopped. Which secret, which one?

"I don't think you are telling me about a real person. Why do I never turn up the right cards or find out what she is thinking? For all I know, she is just someone you've invented, or it's another way of talking about yourself. That has happened to me before."

Amalia laughed, in her April coat with the neat collar. "Is that what you think? Marie is my old friend. You have seen her picture. I have centimetre-by-centimetre enlargements of her lungs."

"If she had committed suicide and you were wondering why—I've had cases of that."

"She never will. Marie will go on and on."

"There is your answer—Marie will go on and on. I don't know what you want from me. I can't give you any answers. Go home, Amalia. Never come back here. Go away."

Marie kill herself? You would have to smother Marie; put the whole map of Paris over her face and hold it tight.

Amalia rehearses for her next session with Madame

Gisèle: "I want to show her the slums sometimes, show her my hands, my hair when it isn't dyed, show her what my life has been. It becomes a hysterical film speeded up.... You should see her going to work every morning. She can hardly put one crippled foot down after the other. She goes by two kiosks on her way to the métro station and stops and reads the newspapers. She comes to dinner every Sunday, bringing a bottle of champagne and a box of pastry—her crooked finger under the pink bow-knot on the box. She brings the first strawberries, the first melon in summer, the first lilacs; she smiles and tells about her work, her letters from the Americans; she says she went to the Opéra-Comique—she is fond of 'Louise' —and she smiles and we see her teeth. She brings cigarettes for Dino. She has never asked for an account. Dino has it ready, but she has never asked. You would think something had been settled for Marie, sorted out a long time ago."

Amalia thinks they might forgive Marie if she insulted them—if she stamped her foot, called them liars and cheats. She could have their respect that way. Failing respect, she might still have their pity. "Weep," they would tell her. "Admit you are no luckier than we are, that every move was a mistake, that you are one of the dead. Be one of us, and be loved." Once Marie said, "You should have had children, Amalia. *Émigrés* need them; otherwise they die of suffocation." She thinks they need a repository for their hopes and dreams. What about her own? "Make a wish," Marie will say, as if there was still something to wish for. They ought to do it: put their faces so close they cannot see each other's eyes and say, "We wish—we wish—but first we must know what Marie has wished for us."

VACANCES PAX

❖

❖

MIDSUMMER NIGHT has always been a pagan festival, and the Christians did not change its nature by naming the day for St John the Baptist. In Scandinavian countries the sun does not set and people behave immorally. In villages in France and Germany, the same pagan fires are still burned, but they are called *"les feux St Jean"* or *"Johannisfeuer,"* and engaged couples jump over the embers hand in hand and are blessed by the priest.

According to tradition as well as that year's lunar calendar, the twenty-fourth of June should have been dry and clear but turned out to be steamy and hot. Stuart Fenwick had persuaded a tall fat girl named Valerie to come and see the trench where he had planted peanuts. (It took Fenwick to consider this a form of courtship.) Valerie walked before him, on the trodden path between holiday bungalows. She had what seemed to his besotted eyes a Tudor bearing, and was majestic in flowered slacks. She carried a dirty fine-toothed comb.

Two and even three times a day, sitting cross-legged on a plastic raincoat on a terrace she thought was private, she clutched strands of ginger hair with her left hand and combed the wrong way, from the ends to the roots. A matchbox transistor strapped to her wrist relayed Radio Monte Carlo close to her ear as she combed. Fenwick imagined the horrible music as a sort of elastic, now plump, now taut. He was supposed to be going about his business, which was the running of a holiday colony called Vacances Pax, but he parted the cypress hedge to look down on the combing without guilt or haste. It seemed to

191

him a gentle and virginal rite, like weaving. When Valerie gathered the locks that framed her brow, made a fan of them, and placed them tenderly over the rest, allowing no stragglers, no nonsense, it was the final gesture, like biting off a thread.

The vacation colony was a collection of little prefab bungalows going down the terraced side of an arid Maritime Alp just behind Grasse. It dated from the early 1950s, when the "One Europe" idea had enormous emotional appeal, and it was thought that all national differences would be dispersed and all prejudices effaced if a few people believing this could be so were to spend their holidays together, talking and exchanging ideas and being decent and kind. Every bungalow flew a different flag, and meals were taken together — the whole colony. On fine days they ate out-of-doors, and when it rained too hard for the cane trellis and grape-vines that were supposed to protect them, they moved into a large bare bungalow used constantly in the old days for meetings and discussions — now only sometimes, if a vacationer wanted to show slides or his own movies. It was a long way from the kitchen, and there were many days of rain.

It had not been easy to get Valerie to come and look at the peanut trench. She was down here in the south of France to rest and recover from an appendectomy — so she said. Far from being the one never to ask questions, Fenwick asked a great many. Her Tudor head-dress covered fragile or perhaps selective ear-drums. She took no notice of his questions.

"Now, that is interesting." She meant a drum-shaped yellow metal box, bearing KLM tags and "Perishable — Keep Cool" in large letters. Several of the Dutch members of the vacation colony were standing in a circle around it. The drum contained herring, which, all chipping in, they had ordered from home as a treat. Whoever brought it here had deposited it in the middle of greenery that he perhaps took to be weeds but that happened to be Fenwick's moss campion, transplanted with devotion from Alpine distance. From the metal drum the smell of fish spread out in widening rings. They were all included — the Dutch, and Fenwick, and Valerie, and Tom Waterford, who had strolled up after them.

"You'll want a tin opener, to start with," Fenwick said.

It turned out that somebody had one. Until now, they had simply been admiring the box. No one was pushy; no one wanted to be first.

Valerie gave the youngest adult a grave nod, as if to say, "I understand and approve." This man, wearing a neat moustache, and with a shirt lightly laid over his sunburn, then crouched down with the tin opener and in a minute bent back the lid.

"Ah, herring," he said, and sighed, and they all looked with solemn pleasure at the dark brine.

"Now, that *is* interesting," said Valerie, perhaps to Fenwick. "Because every herring is the same size, and I think there must be layers."

"A plank!" said the man who had done the opening. He should have been a naval officer. Instead, he was dedicated, by his own choice, to Shell Oil for ever and ever. He eyed Valerie, but received no more encouragement. She had already told Fenwick she came abroad to be not entertained but informed, and Fenwick was beginning to see what she meant. A four-year-old boy ran and fetched the wrong thing, but finally a large, clean plank was found. The man with Shell Oil, whom Fenwick now hated (he also hated the shape of the drum, thinking Valerie might compare it with his), cleaned several of the fish and cut them into fillets. The first went to a little girl. She tipped back her head, held the fillet between two fingers, and swallowed like a seal. Then everyone had some, as fast as the young man could clean them. Presently, their tongues swollen and thick, the Dutch members apologized to Valerie — the herring was too green. They fetched thick slices of fresh bread from the kitchen and made sandwiches, and when that palled, they cut up onions and added those to the bread. At half past twelve, when the gong sounded, the drum was nearly empty, ants were forming battalions to carry off the debris, and the Dutch dispersed to get ready for lunch.

The extraordinary thing was, to Fenwick, that they would eat; they would all of them eat as if they had never seen food in their lives. They came here because it was cheap, because they went everywhere, and they came with no provision for their ferocious sunburns. Their presence in great numbers meant a large meal at noon with boiled potatoes. Afterward, they would drink coffee with milk. No good cook would stay. Fenwick should have presided over this meal, if only to register the complaints, but there were days when he could not watch one more fork break open one more potato, or see how the men loosened their belts or pushed back from the table with a groan. Valerie, reduced to one meal a day because of her figure, accepted the tribute of a sandwich without onions and walked on, Fenwick after her. He had never had Valerie alone, free of Shell Oil, or Tom Waterford, or the children who placed an ear to the wrist-watch radio, their faces rapt.

"In the old days," he said, desiring not only her company but her attention, "Vacances Pax was a noble try. One Europe, no frontiers." He was sorry he had started this; it made him sound ancient. What if he were to say to that tower of red hair, "This is the twenty-fourth of June, and tonight I am going to build a bonfire"? Then, to see if she was listening, "And burn Tom Waterford as an offering to the gods." No, she might choose that moment to hear, and then tell it. They plodded on, slightly out of breath because they were going uphill.

"Do you know what I think?" said Valerie, stopping and stunning him with her full consideration and her soft brown eyes. "I think it was kind of those people to share their fish with us. I can think of a lot of English who wouldn't share—" she hesitated as if consulting a guide for some national dish "—their chocolates."

"You would, though," he said dotingly.

"I never eat anything fattening," she said, with regret, and there was nothing to do but walk on, for he could not see how to move on through this conversation, which seemed enclosed by some special Valerie-minded fence. To court a woman properly, you had to understand not only her feelings, which were less tender than he had been led to think in his youth, but also her mind. Speculations about Valerie's mind occupied him agreeably until they climbed the last steep path and stood before the peanut trench. From below, a man's voice said, "I think I'll skip lunch," and then a crystalline female English voice said, "It's filthy." It sounded like Tom Waterford's wife. Valerie had reached the edge of the trench and was gazing down, waiting to be informed. Fenwick took a step nearer. He began to speak distinctly but with haste, for one of the things he did not know about Valerie's mind was its limit of concentration. "First I had the idea," Fenwick said, "and then, you see, I just started to dig the trench."

Appearing at the herring festival at the last minute, just before the tin was opened, Tom Waterford was given a sandwich and wandered away. He was being especially polite, for the day before he had overheard an extremely unpleasant thing said about him and it had changed his feelings toward the Dutch, who until then had seemed so jolly. He, of the light-blue eyes and hair going grey, had heard, "Good-looking in a conventional English way. Yes, they look as if they might be intelligent, but it is only an appearance, almost a joke." This is what he had heard from the next terrace, and of course knew he was not meant to overhear; if his critics were speaking English it was only because it was the common language of this place and season. The cross-section of Europe he and his wife had been promised had turned out to be English-German-Dutch. What an imposter Fenwick was! What a poseur! Of all the false prophets, those who mixed brotherhood and politics were the worst.... Waterford was for one or the other, each in its place. Coming here had been an idea of his wife's. They tried something new every year. The "European cross-section" had one thing in common: they were all taking a June holiday to escape the summer rush. That put everyone in one basket. But there was a drawback, for it meant having small children about, under school age — the Waterfords had expected none at all. At times, the place was no better than a public nursery. If Tom hated luncheon it was because of the babies, sitting on their mothers' laps, pawing the food on their mothers' plates. The guests ate at trestle-tables — another of Fenwick's ideas. His notions of One Europe all seemed to be connected with food — everyone eating the same thing, everyone chewing. Meg Waterford did not mind the trestle-tables; what she minded was the absence of nannies. She did hate chaos so. She could not hide her feelings. When she talked about juvenile delinquency, her face went dry as paper. Everything retreated — all the humanity, all the blood — and only something that looked like paper was left. They ought to be birched, flogged, she said.

"Tell us about your dogs that bite everybody," said one

of the children at the lunch table. That had to be translated, of course.

Meg smiled, and repeated with clarity, as if asking directions in a foreign capital, "Our — dogs — bite — strangers."

"But only strangers who come to the back door," finished the child. No one minded translating. Perhaps everyone, even the grown people, wanted to hear it. Another subject they liked was Tom, who was a magistrate and could send people to prison for up to six months. Really, Meg was tired of explaining why it was that a man with no legal training had this power. To say "no knowledge of law," as Fenwick once had, was a bit thick, for being a magistrate implied knowing something; you acquired knowledge with the first case that came before you, and from there on it was common sense.

Tom drew near now, sandwich in hand. He was wearing a red-and-white striped shirt and, she thought, a quite astonishing burgundy scarf. He had said something about driving down to Grasse to get something for the twenty-fourth of June bonfire. Matches? What else could it be? She looked once more at this scarf, and went back to what she was saying. She had never in her life remarked on anyone's clothes. She did not know what her husband owned. From time to time a tie or a handkerchief astonished her, that was all.

Tom heard Meg speaking about "Nennie." It was "Nannie," but that was the way Meg spoke. He always had trouble adjusting his ears to a woman's voice, even his wife's, as if to a dialect. He never had that trouble with men. "How she would slap our hands!" said Meg joyously, and imitated the gesture, saying "Slep, slep." Nannie was an ignorant, an uneducated woman — Meg thought it only fair to describe her entirely — now in retirement. She spent her time making shoe-trees and coat-hangers for her former charges. "I save up bits of satin and velvet for her," said Meg, with a tight smile.

When Tom was speaking about Meg, he often said, "She's worth ten of me."

"I think I'll skip lunch," he said now.

"I don't blame you," she chanted, loud and icelike. "It's filthy."

Valerie, Tudor-headed, looked down at the peanut trench. In wet ground, ordinary unroasted peanuts (kind bachelor Fenwick explained) would and did produce roots that were a mass of dry threads, and dark-green leaves that spread like clover. If Valerie liked instructive conversation as much as she said she did, Fenwick was serving it up on a plate. He had now given up the hopes and dreams of years ago, he said, and had schemes that he thought of as vengefully selfish — a grapefruit monopoly, for instance, or the first pineapple plantation in Europe, or a thriving market in avocados. His earlier hopes had failed because they had not sprung from a motive sufficiently sordid; venality equals reality. And so now he raised spindly avocado plants to a height of at least sixteen inches before they died.

"One could make a fortune in limes, too," he said. "Limes grown in Europe."

"Money can't buy love," Valerie remarked, quoting her wrist radio. If she was stating a profound conviction, then Fenwick was on the wrong track. Someone — a singer — had got to her first, and told her that love was to be praised and money decried. What if before that she had heard a song called "Love Can't Buy Money"?

He was about to propose it, when Valerie said placidly. "I don't think the food here is filthy. I think there's just too much of it."

Either her mind spread and darted and flew, too fast for

him to follow, or it tucked its head under its wing and slept. He told her, nevertheless, how in the old days they had all come here for One Europe and had eaten the hated garlic in a spirit approaching good will. There had been peaceful demonstrations. Once, the French-Italian frontier between Menton and Ventimiglia was left open for a few hours, and the whole Pax colony packed up and drove those bumpy miles in the midget rattly cars people had driven when Valerie was a little girl, with "Holland Believes in Europe" streaming from some, and any number of Scandinavian flags. That demonstration, legendary now, was confirmed in photos Fenwick kept in his bungalow. They showed the customs men grinning and waving while all the French sped into Italy to load up on cheap petrol and the Italians swarmed the other way, to get at Fenwick knew not what — perfume and bananas, it turned out. Nobody believed in anything now, he said. The pox-plague of Mediterranean restaurants had their food sent, frozen, from distant parts. You could buy the same salad bowl from San Remo to Marseille. Fenwick received all-Europe products, such as washing powder, with instructions in four languages, and in each of the four languages there would be mistakes in spelling and grammar. They held the universe lightly; it was not Fenwick's fault.

He perceived that he had talked too much, he seldom saw girls any more, except for the inevitable English pair, one a case of sunstroke and one of food poisoning, and no longer knew how to talk to them. And here, this June, was his regal Valerie, burned to a bright pink but not complaining.

She waved her herring sandwich, having stood through this monologue, and perhaps even listened. "What's that thing?"

"A datura."

"Oh." Munching and staring.

"Not a date palm. Nothing to do with dates."

"I know. I've seen a whole forest of date palms in Spain. I've forgotten where. I did see it, though, on a tour."

"If you sleep under a datura tree," said Fenwick, proceeding with his idea of courtship, "you might die."

"Who has? Anyone?"

"Just don't do it."

She threw the rest of the sandwich away and licked her fingers. She said, "If anyone's going down to Grasse or Cannes, I need some things for my transistor."

"I'll take you down a bit later," said Fenwick, staring at her arms. "I've been drying wood for the bonfire. I want to look at it first."

The peanut trench was a gathering place, a watering hole, for now Tom Waterford bobbed up and said, "I'll take you," and the last Fenwick saw of his Tudor queen was her flowered stretch pants as she climbed into the Waterfords' Mini-Minor, head first.

Fenwick was in time to join his guests for coffee. Between the straw mat and the edge of the table a strip of hot metal, a forgotten spoon, stung his wrist. Meg Waterford was talking about animals. "I love wild animals—tigers," she said, as if she had often been contradicted, as if all wild animals were to be taken away from her. A German told of having seen on television tons of strawberries ruined by hail somewhere, and farmers crying. Telling it, he could not keep his voice steady. Fenwick, mourning his beloved, left them—they were all getting on so well. They sounded like the ingenious all-Europe programs in which the best drummer from Denmark performs from a studio in Copenhagen, along with a trumpet from Stuttgart, an electric guitar from Milan and France's finest clarinet. No musician can hear or see the others, for each is in his home city, but owing to the competence of sound technicians, they can be heard all playing "Dinah" at the same time.

Fenwick began to gather together wood and the dried herbs and plants for tonight's fire; he could still believe in magic. He needed seven elements to make the fire succeed, but they were woods found in the North. He would have to settle for rosemary, broom — whatever was sweet-smelling and would burn. Valerie might be induced to leap over the ashes. A fertility rite, but Fenwick would tell her it was for peace, harmony — anything that might appeal to her sleeping or soaring mind. The thought of great Valerie leaping cheered him.

"I do believe you are some sort of Druid," Meg called to him from the table.

"No, no," said Fenwick, "only a bard."

He began piling the dried herbs with some perception of happiness, all the while listening to Meg telling the others that she had lost, somewhere, once, long ago, in a place she could not remember, a really valuable ring.

A REPORT

❖

❖

"THE boots are not authentic," says M Monnerot. "Authentic boots must exist somewhere, but I have never found them — at least not in my size. Everything else seems real."

He stands with his hands on his hips, scowling at himself in the glass. He wears the uniform of a Waffen S.S. superior officer, but the effect is patchy, and for a good reason — the components of the uniform were bought separately. Willi has no emotional feeling about the uniform whatsoever, but his sense of order is offended by the decorations. No soldier could possibly have been simultaneously on so many fronts, and if you look closely you can see that some of the ribbons are not even German. M Monnerot is an impostor, though he looks impressive. Next to him, a man in civilian clothes appears ridiculous. Willi, the civilian, looks as if he exercised some marginal trade, such as photographing tourists as they come out of the Louvre, or asking thirty selected families how often they clean their shoes; but he is a translator, entrusted with difficult and often secret texts, at the rate of eleven centimes a word.

M Monnerot is small of eye; he pulls the cap sideways and down so that his gaze is shadowed. According to one of the detectives who have been following him (his wife is trying to obtain evidence for a divorce), he is handsomer in uniform than Himmler, whose picture hangs on the wall, but not nearly so effective as Heydrich, who strides beside Himmler. Heydrich's greatcoat swirls, his arm swings; the whole sense of the picture seems to be menace and movement. He wears a sword. M Monnerot is on the look-out for one like it. Swords are easy enough to find, but every time he buys one he compares it with the photograph and some detail seems at fault. Could it be that Heydrich had a sword specially made for himself? Willi, questioned, shakes his head. It could be true; it seems to him that during his childhood in Germany he heard opposing opinions — for instance, his mother believed that very high-up Party members spent rather a lot on their own adornment, but his father knew better, and maintained that every pfennig of tax collected was somehow or other returned to the people.

Upon M Monnerot's table, folded, are two red, black and white flags. One came from the Flea Market, where several merchants now make a specialty of Nazi souvenirs, and is said to have flown high in Kiev. There is no way of proving it, but as it may have come such a long way, he paid more for it than he would have for any of the others.

He turns to Willi and says, "I am not blaming you, but I don't think the flag *you* sold me is authentic."

Of course it is not. When Willi was asked for a flag he said they only existed in films; and when M Monnerot insisted, first wheedling, then raising his price to three hundred francs, Willi went to the Bon Marché department store and bought red, black and white bunting and made a passable flag. His first try was nearly a failure — he had his swastika running counter-clockwise. He had to unstitch it and sew it twice. He soaked the flag in salt water and let it dry, then dipped the flag, folded, into a solution of Javelle water. Thus, battle-marked and travel-marked, the flag was welcomed by M Monnerot, and envied by some of his friends, who are also collectors.

"The size of the swastika seems wrong," M Monnerot now complains. 'I don't know why, but when you compare it with some others — a friend of mine pointed it out to me."

Willi says solemnly, "The Kiev flag must have been made after 1942. In 1942 the size was standardized. Now you have one of each."

"You are right," says M Monnerot. "I have one of each."

Willi would like to share this joke with someone, but with whom? He is in the confidence of M Monnerot's wife, and knows she is having her husband followed. She is hoping to catch him at something, but so far he has been careful: he has never stayed out overnight, and never brought a woman into his house — he knows better. "I respect my wife," he has often told Willi, "and her part of my life is sacred." Willi knows that although Mme Monnerot might enjoy the story about the flag she could make trouble for Willi later on. She might be so enraged to think of her husband spending money foolishly that she could not resist telling him. Willi knows, from experience, that mortal enemies often end up in each other's arms. Also, if M Monnerot keeps his mistress out of his home, it is simply because she has a place of her own, rue du Commerce. Part of the detective's report describes how M Monnerot has to fight for parking space on that busy street — how he tries to intimidate his opponent without actually coming to blows. He becomes so red in the face that the author of the report thinks he might die of a stroke one of these days. Willi knows more than the detective, but he keeps his information to himself. Perhaps he could sell what he knows — but no; the truth is, he doesn't trust any of these people an inch.

He has seen the latest report, which begins, "The situation has not changed. M Monnerot leaves his office on the stroke of twelve and, after fetching his car in the garage behind the Madeleine, drives in the thick of midday traffic to the corner of the avenue Émile Zola and the rue du Commerce. As he can never find a place along the curb, he leaves his Ariane double- and even triple-parked while he buys two small filet steaks, or one lean entrecôte. At the greengrocer he buys two apples or two bananas. Occasionally he omits the fruit and walks half a block to buy two vanilla yoghurts. He pays cash everywhere and is not known to have any debts. Recently he obtained control of a dry-cleaning establishment, rue du Commerce, which he wanted to name Mon Pressing. However as there are four establishments by that name in the telephone book he has changed his mind, and the sign now reads Pressing Brigitte. M Monnerot has a valid reason for his daily trips to the Émile Zola-rue du Commerce area of the city."

Willi could add that the apartment on the rue du Commerce where M Monnerot has his share of the steak, fruit or yoghurt was occupied from May to July by Fräulein Ilse (Bobbie) Bauer, born of a French corporal with the Army of Occupation and a seventeen-year-old German bilingual stenographer, in Coblenz, May 5th, 1947. Before taking up residence in the rue du Commerce, Bobbie was *au pair* cook, housemaid, laundress and governess in the home of M and Mme Laurent, their daughters Chantal and Eliane, baby Charles and grey poodle Tisane. Bobbie had a room on the sixth floor of the apartment building, along with the servants working for other families, and students to whom the rooms were rented at two hundred francs a month. Some rooms contained clandestine Spanish families, one member of which—wife, sister, fiancée —was employed as a maid, and who, by means of mattresses piled in the daytime and distributed on the floor at night, was able to house four or five persons in a room already filled by a single bed, a chair and a wardrobe. The students have their meals at the university restaurants, and the space taken in the Spanish rooms by alcohol stoves and saucepans is devoted, in their chambers, to a record-player and the records of Jacques Brel, Georges Brassens, Barbara, Guy Béart and Bob Dylan.

Although she was nauseated by the smell of cooking oil from the Spanish quarters, and disturbed by the records in the students' rooms, Bobbie spent her evenings upstairs. The Laurents had never invited her to share their television. Because her mother had borne her at the age of seventeen, Bobbie was afraid to go out alone until after her eighteenth birthday. Once another girl took her to the Select, in Montparnasse, where she met Willi. She told him about the Laurents, and that on the sixth floor there was one toilet, Turkish style, without a lock, and one basin with a cold-water tap, and that her favorite poet was Lamartine. Willi advised her to go home to Coblenz. She said she could not until she had learned enough French to become a bilingual stenographer; her mother had married a man who was interested in Bobbie, and (showing off her French) she was *de trop* at home.

On her eighteenth birthday, her French hosts invited her to watch a film on television. The program was already under way when she arrived. She slipped into a chair. Eliane and Chantal sat cross-legged on the floor, rapt, though the white wobbling square on the lower left-hand corner of the screen was an official warning that the program was not recommended for children. M and Mme Laurent did not turn their heads when Bobbie entered the room. Bobbie was extremely puzzled and depressed by the film, which had no action whatever, but showed ugly, unkempt, naked women standing in a field of tall grass, in a disorderly queue. She believed it at first to be a film about prehistoric people; she thought it could be some lost tribe in a jungle, perhaps in South America. The jumpy light and abrupt camera movements suggested the scene had been filmed from the wrong distance, and by an amateur. Presently the image changed to an abstract design of white faintly striated in grey, which, when the picture became sharper, was seen to be a pile of bodies. As Bobbie half rose from her chair, M and Mme Laurent swung away from the screen. She saw their profiles, then their faces. Mme Laurent said bitterly, "*You* did this," and her husband said, "If it wasn't you, it was your father."

Bobbie left the room, ran down the stairs and walked in the spring night as far as the Trocadéro. The fountains were playing. A number of tourists took pictures of the Eiffel Tower and the lighted water. M Monnerot, who was on his way to dine with a friend from out of town at Le Petit Marguery, and had stopped at the Trocadéro to admire the view, discovered Bobbie without her purse, without her coat, without her identity card or passport, and without a key to get back into the Laurents' apartment house. She was weeping bitterly. After a short conversation during which she shook her head several times, she joined the two men for dinner.

The apartment on the rue du Commerce — as Mme Monnerot knows — was bought, as an investment, by M Monnerot's unmarried sister, who lives in Lyon and never goes near the place. Nevertheless, the telephone is in her name, and the gas, light and water (though the bills are paid by successive tenants) are in her name, too. No tenant has ever been given a lease to sign, and the concierge is bribed. Bobbie moved in as one more incarnation of M Monnerot's sister. The arrangement lasted less than two months. Fräulein Bauer was frightened by M Monnerot — no one knows why. She made the mistake of calling M Monnerot at his office, and the greater mistake of calling him at his home. That telephone call was, in fact, the beginning of Mme Monnerot's suspicions, and the reason she began receiving detectives' reports. By the time the detectives began working, however, Bobbie had disappeared. Someone told Willi she was seen with a suitcase around the Gare de l'Est. Perhaps she followed his advice and went home. The official report knows only this: "M Monnerot's sister's apartment is occupied by Mlle Brigitte Vanderplank, who is a French citizen. Mlle Vanderplank works for a wholesale dress firm as hostess and model when coats and dresses are shown to buyers in Belgium, Luxembourg, Holland and Switzerland. She is twenty-four, and speaks French, Flemish and several German dialects. It is to her apartment that M Monnerot takes his daily steak et cetera. Sometimes he and Mlle Vanderplank meet and shop together. In that case she chooses the food and he pays. He sometimes allows her to drive. When the car is parked to his satisfaction he rushes to open the door for Mlle Vanderplank, helps her out and kisses her hand. M Monnerot has told a few friends that he is on close terms with a young countess who belongs to a family from the northern part of France. Mlle Vanderplank wears an apple-green suit and white shoes. She carries a white purse with a gold chain. She has been described variously as 'exquisite,' 'undernourished,' 'common,' 'distinguished,' but all are agreed that she has blond hair. M Monnerot has told Mlle Vanderplank that he was a secret agent in the last war, and also with the paratroops. Mlle Vanderplank has been heard to say that her landlady's brother (as she correctly describes him) is a decent citizen; his patriotism is unquestioned; he believes in republican institutions; he detests the Americans, the British, the Russians, the Chinese, and he despises the Germans for having been defeated in the last war. Some time ago Mlle Vanderplank asked for a lease 'to show her parents,' who, she said, were concerned about her housing arrangements. M Monnerot drew up a lease, and filled out several 'receipts' for the monthly rent. Mlle Vanderplank had the lease and receipts photocopied in the presence of two trusted friends, one of them a solicitor, and returned the originals to M Monnerot, who tore them up."

What do you think?" said Mme Monnerot when Willi had read the report. Willi seems to her the very bastion of common sense. He may be ready to sacrifice his principles, but no one can say what his principles are. He does not appear venal. He is extremely discreet, and no trouble to women.

Willi sticks to the information in the report. He speaks like a rational machine. He tells her that, one, M Monnerot has not commited an offence that can be proved. Two, she has no grounds for a divorce. Three, Mlle Vanderplank is the legal tenant of the apartment (though the landlady's brother has yet to discover this) and has photocopies of receipts.

"Is there anything you know and are not telling me?" she pleads.

"No," says Willi. "All I have is an enlarged photograph of an officer's sword, which he said he wanted."

"Then nothing can ever change," says Mme Monnerot.

"No, nothing," says Willi, which might be the expression of a more general belief.

"He is odious," she says. "Why do you waste time doing favours for him?"

"Oh — you know," says Willi vaguely.

He thinks to himself, One, I need the money. Two, it stops him from nagging. Three, I am not sure; I must be expecting something.

Expecting what? He sees the faked flag, the dead decorations, the symbols counter-clockwise, and feels bewildered, as if he had been given permission to laugh. "Tell him," he says, and breaks down. He cannot stop laughing. It is disgraceful; he sees Mme Monnerot is offended. He cannot stop, and begins to weep. "Tell him," he says, when he can draw breath, "tell him I'll look for the boots."

The Sunday
After Christmas

❖

❖

AT a quarter to four the sun moved behind a mountain. The valley below us went dark, as if an enormous bird had just spread its wings. For a moment I understood what my mother means when she complains I give her the feeling of being outside life. The two of us, and the American girl my mother had picked up, were still on the terrace between the ski-lift and a restaurant. I saw, as the lights of the restaurant welled up, how the girl looked quickly, wistfully almost, at the steamed windows and the hissing coffee machine.

"Don't you want to go in?" said my mother's new friend. "It's kind of cold now the sun's gone."

My mother made a wild, gay movement of turning to me, as if this were only one of a hundred light-hearted decisions we made together. It is extraordinary how, in Italy, she becomes the eccentric Englishwoman — hair flying, sunglasses askew, too friendly with the waiter at breakfast, but unexpectedly waspish if a child brushes against her chair: "Harold, didn't you notice? The little brute deliberately barged into me!" An hour later she will be ready to tell the little brute my life's story and what I was like when I was his age. Her greed for people makes her want to seem attractive to almost anyone — a child, or a waiter, or this girl, whose absence of charm and mystery made her seem, to me, something like a large coloured poster. My mother dreads being alone with me. In the last of the afternoon, when she suddenly says, "You must be cold," meaning that she is, and we gather everything together and start the slow progression back to the hotel, I sense her panic. The

217

dark minutes between afternoon and night creep by; she looks surreptitiously at her watch; she imagines she has been walking beside me down a twilit street for years on end. To engage and hold my attention on the way home she will comment on everything she sees — the patches of snow so curiously preserved on a shutter, the late skiers in the distance like matchstick figures, the expressiveness of those matchsticks. "Look," she says, at red berries, green moss, beeches, a juniper, reeds frozen in a black stream, the plumed grasses above the snow. I am not an old man in a fur-lined pelisse; she is not pushing me along in a wheel-chair (I may, in fact, be carrying her skis); I am not snow-blind. I must be all those things in her eyes. I am crippled, aged, in the dark, an old man she diverts with the crumbs of life because part of him is dying, and even a partial death is like her own. "Why don't you talk to me?" she used to say. She is past that kind of pleading now. She knows that I can hear her thinking, so that speech isn't needed. To answer the silent sentences in her mind, I answer, "Yes, but if that little old man died, you would at least be free, wouldn't you?"

"Oh, Harold," she replies. "Your father *is* dead, darling, and he was never old."

It had rained until shortly before Christmas. There was deep snow only on the upper slopes, which were marked *"difficile"* on the map in our hotel. We took the chair-lift to the very top every day and came down at four o'clock. I heard her telling her newest American friend how she used to come to this village years ago, with my father, without me. She could remember electric cars shaped like the swan boats she used to be taken for rides in when she was a child. She would have liked to ski all the way down to the village, but hardly anyone did. The runs were too short, broken by stone walls and the boundaries of close-set trees, and lower down no snow at all except on a mule path, which was hard and icy and followed the course of a mountain stream. She would have tried it, she said, had there been anyone to go with. She was not confident enough alone. Suppose she were to fracture a leg and lie for hours without help? At fifty a break is a serious matter; she might never walk without limping again. Her hands shook as she lighted the girl's cigarette and then her own.

"Harold sits for hours, as long as there's sun," she said. "He doesn't feel heat or cold. He wanted marvellous equipment; now he won't use it. I don't insist."

The new girl, who had said her name was Sylvia, pulled off her knitted cap. Her hair, dark, fell over the shoulders of a white sweater. An exchange of intimate gossip, my mother's alternative to friendship, was under way. The girl said quite easily, "There doesn't seem to be any friction between you two, but my mother never lets me alone. I've travelled with her sometimes and it's no joke. She drinks too much and she gets loud. She'll have her breakfast in the bar and ask the bartender a whole lot of questions — things she wouldn't do at home."

"I think I'm always the same," my mother cried — like something screamed at a party.

"I am sorry for her," the girl went on. "She needs all of somebody's life and she hasn't ever had that."

"Not even your father's?"

"He looked after her, but he didn't give her all his life. No one has the right to a whole extra life." Her pure, humourless regard rested on each of us. Her look preached to us; one of us was being warned. "I lived with her for a year after my father died. I've got to leave her now. I came all this way just so as not to spend Christmas at home. She's got to get used to it. It's a sort of shock treatment."

"Well, that's very strong of you," said my mother. "Isn't

that so, Harold? But are you really leaving so soon? Can't you stay until after New Year's Eve? You may never be here again."

I could hear her thinking, *Don't go. Stay. Are two or three days so much to give me? You gave your mother a year.*

I love my mother and I don't care two pins about you, I heard the girl answer.

She said, "No, I've got to get back."

I looked at the lights strung along the street, and the lights slowly moving out of the car park at the foot of the lift. I saw the girl shiver, as if she felt that great wing rushing over the valley.

"I can't go down," I said.

"Of course you can't," said my mother. Her little apricot face looked cheerful. "We're going down in the lift."

I said, "I can't go down in the chair either. I can't go down at all."

"It's mountain sickness," said my mother, making roundabout movements with her cigarette, as if to show what vertigo means. "It will be over in a minute. It just means a wait. What a bother for you!" She was taking it for granted, of coure, that the girl would not feel free to leave us there.

"Shouldn't we go in?" said the girl, again attracted by the warm light.

"He'll want to stay out, I'm afraid."

"Oh. Well, we can have coffee, anyway," said the girl. "We're all freezing." She went into the restaurant and I saw her leaning on the counter, fingering chocolate bars, wishing she had never talked to us. A ski club from Turin filled the place. They were noisy as monkeys, ordering hot drinks and food and combing their hair before a little mirror. I saw the girl smiling at them, waiting for the coffee, but they were too full of themselves to notice a stranger.

"I don't believe this," my mother said to me. "There's nothing wrong with you today. You're perfectly well. You're shamming, shamming." Her voice broke on her habit of repeating the same word twice. She was disappointed as a child over the girl. I tried to reason with her: Was Sylvia her real name? It did not seem an American name to me; it was, in fact, the name of one of my aunts. But by now my mother had left me and joined the girl. I could see her back, and the girl's face. On the counter was a tray and three cups. My mother was telling her about me: "He had an unusual experience, you know," she was saying. "He was one of a group of university students visiting a large hospital. While they were waiting for their conducted tour, a nurse told Harold that the place was run by a most eccentric doctor who did experiments on children and on young people, and that Harold and his friends were the new victims. The patients, when they survived, were so changed in character that they were no longer fit for life in the outside world. 'Didn't you notice the scars on the necks of the little boys playing football outside?' the nurse said. She advised him not to fight, as there was nothing he could do. Harold argued for his freedom. His argument centred on two things — that he was young and had a right to live, and that he still hadn't decided what he wanted to do, and needed time to find out. It seemed impossible to him that she shouldn't understand this. She was a serious person — a nice girl. They went outside and sat discussing his life on a bench overlooking the playing field. Suddenly, in a second, it was clear that the nurse had been convinced by Harold's arguments and had purposely brought him out-of-doors, and, just as he understood, she said, 'Run for it.' His reflexes are very slow, but he must have pulled himself together, and he did run, through the players, to liberty, and the road outside, and to his own home — safe, safe."

She bobbed her head as she repeated the last word. I did not think, or guess, or imagine what she was saying; I *knew*. She must have then said, "Pretend it is funny," because the girl laughed, and was still remembering her laughter as she picked up the tray and brought it out to me.

My mother said, "I was telling Sylvia about that midnight Mass where they had the live animals, and how the priest said the goat was an incarnation of the Devil and had to be taken out, and then the goat broke loose, and all the villagers said later they had seen the Devil, really seen him, with his flaming eyes."

"I wish I had seen that," said the girl, with a lift to the sentence, as if it were half a question, as if giving me a reason to speak. I was already thinking about the trip down, and the slight sighing of the cable.

"He's fine now," my mother said.

Below, because it was Sunday, everyone except the visitors looked awkward and solemn. It seemed an unnatural day, that had to be lived through in formal, festive clothes. The men wore thick moustaches turned up at the ends, and black felt hats, and knee breeches. They looked distinguished and calm, and not like any idea the girl had ever had about Italians, I heard her say. She drew near my mother. She repeated that she had not known before coming here that Italians could be patient, or naturally elegant, any more than she had known they possessed an educated middle class. In her mind (she had not really given it thought) she had been coming to a Rossellini, a De Sica country.

While she was saying this, she was also saying to me,

222

Was it a dream? Did you really have an experience like that? If it was a dream, why didn't she say so?

I answered, "It was a long experience, lasting well over a year."

"Harold, Harold!" my mother said, looking not at me but at the girl. We had reached the girl's hotel, and the long goodbye my mother would now insist upon would be, in her eyes, one minute's friendship more. "Are you leaving because there isn't enough snow?" she said. "There will be a Mass for snow on New Year's Eve. All the hotel owners and all the shopkeepers are contributing, they say." In my mother's poor, immediate vision of future events (never more than three or four days in span), she and her new friend walked in moonlight. Vega was bright and blue as a diamond; their shadows were hard and black as if cut out with knives.

"The goat, of course, the goat," I said. "'Don't move,' I said to Mother. 'When he sees the Cross he's sure to panic.'"

"I never move anyway," said my mother to Sylvia, to prolong the goodbye. "Nothing makes *me* move." She smiled, and even when the girl had turned aside forever, kept the smile alive.

APRIL FISH

❖

❖

BECAUSE I was born on the first day of April, I was given April as a Christian name. Here in Switzerland they make Avril of it, which sounds more like a sort of medicine than a month of spring. "Take a good dose of Avril," I can imagine Dr Ehrmann saying, to each of the children. Today was the start of the fifty-first April. I woke up early and sipped my tea, careful not to disturb the dogs sleeping on the foot of the bed on their own Red Cross blanket. I still have nightmares, but the kind of terror has changed. In the hanging dream I am no longer the victim. Someone else is hanged. Last night, in one harrowing dream, one of my own adopted children drowned, there, outside the window, in the Lake of Geneva. I rushed about on the grass, among the swans. I felt dew on my bare feet; the hem of my velvet dressing gown was dark with it. I saw very plainly the children's toys: the miniature tank Igor has always wanted, and something red—a bucket and spade, perhaps. My hair came loose and tumbled down my back. I can still feel the warmth and the comfort of it. It was auburn, leaf-coloured, as it used to be. I think I saved Igor; the memory is hazy. I seemed very competent and sure of my success. As I sat in bed, summing up my progress in life as measured by dreams, trying not to be affected by the sight of the rain streaming in rivulets from the roof (I was not depressed by the rain, but by the thought that I could rely on no one, *no one*, to get up on the roof and clear out the weeds and grass that have taken root and are choking the gutter), the children trooped in. They are home for Easter, all three— Igor, with his small thief's eyes, and Robert, the mulatto,

227

who will not say *"Maman"* in public because it makes him shy, and Ulrich, whose father was a famous jurist and his mother a brilliant, beautiful girl but who will never be anything but dull and Swiss. There they were, at the foot of the bed, all left behind by careless parents, dropped like loose buttons and picked up by a woman they call *Maman.*

"Bon anniversaire," said Igor, looking, already, like any postal clerk in Moscow, and the two others muttered it in a ragged way, like a response in church. They had brought me a present, an April fish, but not made of chocolate. It was the glass fish from Venice everyone buys, about twenty inches long, transparent and green — the green of geranium leaves, with chalky white stripes running from head to tail. These children have lived in my house since infancy, but their taste is part of their skin and hearts and fingernails. The nightmare I ought to be having is a projection into the future, a vision of the girls they will marry and the houses they will have — the glass coffee-tables and the Venetian-glass fish on top of the television, unless that space has already been taken up with a lump of polished olive root.

Igor advanced and put the fish down very carefully on the table beside me, and, as he could think of nothing else, began again, *"Bon anniversaire, Maman."* They had nothing to tell me. Their feet scuffled and scratched on the floor — the rug, soiled by the dogs, was away being cleaned.

"What are you going to do today?" I said.

"Play," said Robert, after a silence.

A morning concert struck up on the radio next to me, and I looked for something — an appreciation, a reaction to the music — in their eyes, but they had already begun pushing each other and laughing, and I knew that the music would soon be overlaid by a second chorus, from me, "Don't touch. Don't tease the dogs," all of it negative and as bad for them as for me. I turned down the music and said, "Come and see the birthday present that came in the mail this morning. It is a present from my brother, who is your uncle." I slipped on my reading glasses and spread the precious letter on the counterpane. "It is an original letter written by Dr Sigmund Freud. He was a famous doctor, and that is his handwriting. Now I shall teach you how to judge from the evidence of letters. The writing paper is ugly and cheap — you all see that, do you? — which means that he was a miser, or poor, or lacked aesthetic feeling, or did not lend importance to worldly matters. The long pointed loops mean a strong sense of spiritual values, and the slope of the lines means a pessimistic nature. The margin widens at the bottom of the page, like the manuscript of Keats's 'Ode to a Nightingale.' You remember that I showed you a photograph of it? Who remembers? Ulrich? Good for Ulrich. I means that Dr Freud was the same kind of person as Keats. Keats was a poet, but he died. Dr Freud is also dead. I am sorry to say that the signature denotes conceit. But he was a great man, quite right to be sure of himself."

"What does the letter say?" said Igor, finally.

"It is not a letter written to me. It is an old letter — see the date? It was sent about thirty years before any of you was born. It was written probably to a colleague — look, I am pointing. To another doctor. Perhaps it is an opinion about a patient."

"Can't you read what it says?" said Igor.

I tried to think of a constructive answer, for "I can't read German" was too vague. "Someday you, and Robert, and even Ulrich will read German, and then you will read the letter, and we shall all know what Dr Freud said to his colleague. I would learn German," I went on, "if I had more time."

As proof of how little time I have, three things took place all at once: my solicitor, who only rings up with bad news, called from Lausanne, Maria-Gabriella came in to remove the breakfast tray, and the dogs woke up and began to bark. Excessive noise seems to affect my vision; I saw the room as blurry and one-dimensional. I waved to Maria-Gabriella — discreetly, for I should never want the children to feel *de trop* or rejected — and she immediately understood and led them away from me. The dogs stopped barking, all but poor blind old Sarah, who went on calling dismally into a dark private room in which she hears a burglar. Meanwhile, Maître Gossart was telling me, from Lausanne, that I was not to have one of the Vietnam children. None of them could be adopted; when their burns have healed, they are all to be returned to Vietnam. That was the condition of their coming. He went on telling it in such a roundabout way that I cut him off with "Then I am not to have one of the burned children?" and as he still rambled I said, "But I want a little girl!" I said, "Look here, I want one of the Vietnam babies and I want a girl." The rain was coming down harder than ever. I said, "Maître, this is a filthy, rotten, bloody country, and if it weren't for the income tax I'd pack up and leave. Because of the income tax I am not free. I am compelled to live in Switzerland."

Maria-Gabriella found me lying on the pillows with my eyes full of tears. As she reached for the tray, I wanted to say, "Knock that fish off the table before you go, will you?" but it would have shocked her, and puzzled the boys had they come to learn of it. Maria-Gabriella paused, in fact, to admire the fish, and said, "They must have saved their pocket-money for weeks." It occurred to me then that *poisson d'avril* means a joke, it means playing an April-fool joke on someone. No, the fish is not a joke. First of all, none of them has that much imagination, the fish was too expensive, and, finally, they wouldn't dare. To tell the truth, I don't really want them. I don't even want the Freud letter. I wanted the little Vietnam girl. Yes, what I really want is a girl with beautiful manners, I have wanted her all my life, but no one will ever give me one.

THE CAPTIVE NIECE

❖

❖

WITHOUT the slightest regard for her feelings or the importance of this day, he had said, "Bring back a sandwich or some bread and pâté, will you, anything you see —oh, and the English papers." He spoke as if she were going out on a common errand or an ordinary walk—to look at the Eiffel Tower, for instance. A telephone dangled on the wall just above his head; all he had to do was reach. It was true that her hotel gave no meals except breakfast, but he might have made a show of trying. He lay on the bed and watched her preparing for the interview. Her face in the bathroom mirror seemed frightened and small. She gave herself eyes and a mouth, and with them an air of decision. Knowing he was looking on made her jumpy; she kicked the bathroom door shut, but then, as though fearing a reprimand, opened it gently.

He took no notice, no more than her aunt had ever taken of her tantrums, and when she came, repentant, tearful almost, to kiss him goodbye, he simply held out the three postcards he had been writing—identical views of the Seine for his children in England. How could he? There was only one reason—he was evil and jealous and trying to call thunderbolts down on her head. An old notion of economy prevented her from throwing the cards out the window—they were stamped, and stamps seemed for some reason more precious than coins. "I don't *want* them," she said. Her hand struck nervously on the bottle of wine beside the bed.

"No, that's dangerous," he said quickly, thinking he saw what she was up to. She was something of a thrower, not at him, but away from him, and always with the same intention—to make him see he had, in some way, slighted her. As he might have done with a frantic puppy, he diverted her with a pack of cigarettes and the corkscrew.

"I don't want them, leave me alone!" she cried, and flung them out the open window into the court. "This is your fault," she said, "and now you've got nothing to smoke." But he had a whole carton of cigarettes, bought on the plane, the day before.

He had to console her. "I know," he said, "I know. But do bring another corkscrew, will you? I really can't use my teeth."

Oh, she would pay him out! For this, and for the past and for failing to see her as she was.

Hours later he was exactly as she had left him — reading, under a torn red lampshade, on the ashy bed. The room smelled of smoke and hot iron radiators. You would not have known that a woman had ever lived in it. The first thing she did was open the window, but the air was cold and the rain too noisy, and she had to close it again. He did not say, "Oh, it's you," or "There you are," or anything that might infuriate her and set her off again. He said, as if he remembered what her day had been about, "How did it go?"

She had no desire except to win his praise. "Leget wants me," she said. "I don't mean for this film, but another next summer. He's getting me a teacher for French and a teacher only for French diction. What do you think of *that*? He said it was a pity I had spoken English all my life, because it's so bad for the teeth. Funny that Aunt Freda never thought of it—she was so careful about most things."

"You could hardly have expected her to bring you up in

a foreign language," he said. "She was English. Millions of people speak English."

"Yes, and look at them!" She had never heard about the effects of English until today, but it was as if she had known it forever. She could see millions and millions of English-speaking people—black, Asian and white—each with a misshapen upper jaw. Like her Aunt Freda, he had never been concerned. She gave him a look of slight pity. "Well, it's happened," she went on. "I shall be working in Paris, really working, and with *him*." She untied her damp head scarf and unbuttoned her coat. "When I am R and F that coat will be lined with mink," she said. "Coat sixteen guineas, lining six thousand." R and F meant rich and famous. His response was usually "When I am old and ill and poor..." She remembered that he was ill, and she had not brought him his sandwich. She dropped on her knees beside the bed. "Are you all right? Feeling better?" The poor man lay there with an attack of lumbago —at least she supposed that was what it was. He had never been unwell before, not for a second. Perhaps he had put something out of joint carrying his things at the airport, but that seemed unlikely. He had come with just one small case and a typewriter, as if he were meeting her for the weekend instead of for life.

"I'm all right," he said. "Tell me about Leget."

She stammered, "He thinks I've got...something. A presence. He said that the minute he saw me, when I walked in...He said he had been hoping to talk to me, alone—to talk about me."

"Clever man," he said. "I don't blame him. I know what he means—I saw it when you were seventeen. It's more than a face, more than drive. I thought then that I'd never been close to it before."

The child in her, told it was singular, felt a rush of love.

She said with new urgency, "Are you better? Oh, I forgot to say...he asked who had brought me up. I told him I had no parents. He asked who was, well, *responsible* for me."

"Did you tell him?"

"Of course. I said, my aunt."

"Your aunt! Did you happen to mention she was dead?"

"I told him she'd died reaching for a drink, and how she was born pickled, and how her mind had never been original or sharp, but I loved her and owed her so much. She taught me how to sit and walk and move. Leget said, 'Yes, but your general culture'—don't make a face, darling, it's not the same in French. I told him it was just old detective stories and that the time before I was born seemed a lovely summer day full of detectives rushing to save pretty girls. I never thought about love. I used to just think, When I meet the nice detective..."

He had heard this many times. "Let me know when you do meet him," he said.

"Perhaps you won't like me when I'm R and F," she said. "so it won't matter what I tell you. Perhaps you'd rather I just stayed what you called me once, Aunt Freda's captive niece. You're sick of hearing about her. You're already sick of Leget, and I'm absolutely certain you're sick of me."

He got up by rolling on his side and gripping the edge of the mattress. He was dressed except for his trousers, and in the abjection of pain did not mind looking foolish. He took his jacket off and as he did so heard the lining tear. He stood looking at the bookshelf nailed beside the bed, giving his attention to the tattered Penguins, and *Sélections du Reader's Digest,* out of which Gitta proposed to improve her French. He looked at the Beaujolais he could not open, and the empty bottle of Haig. He said, and meant it now, "I am old and ill and poor." He was thirty-nine. What seems to the traveller ten or twenty years, he remembered, may in real time be ten thousand. In the nineteen years Gitta will have to travel before she overtakes me—but she never will, not unless the lumbago turns out to be fatal. He was old and ill, and he would be poor because he would give everything from now on to his wife and children. He would never buy drink again except in duty-free airport shops. "I'll have to do a hell of a lot of travelling," he remarked.

"What? Oh, you're being silly. Please sit down. Or lie down. Or take something."

"It's the same if I stand." He began to explain that the aspirin he had swallowed earlier would not dissolve because he had nothing to wash it down with; and that pain was lodged like fish-hooks beneath the skin. "But I'll take one more aspirin," he said, to appease Gitta rather than the pain.

She was barely listening, looking intently now at the dark rain, or at her face on the window. She must have been recalling her triumph—her conquest. Turning to him slowly she said, "Why do you have your shirt tucked in that way? It looks funny." She added, "I've never seen anyone else do that."

"You've been knocking around with a lot of damn foreigners in Paris," he said. "Don't even know how to keep their clothes on."

She came to him, awkwardly for a girl who had been taught how to move, and touched his head for fever. "It's nothing. You aren't sick at all." Pain stuck to fragrance like glue; the scent of her hand became a source of uneasiness. Had he really expected to keep her to himself? He knew of one anguish, and that was the separation from his children; but Gitta had been a child, and more— they had been lovers since she was seventeen. He found the aspirin in an open suitcase and hobbled to the bathroom. Clutching the basin, he stood on one foot and flexed his knee.

"Is it that bad?" she said, without sympathy because his forehead was cool. "You're making a horrible face." He looked, as if he had only one minute left, at the walls, which seemed newly papered, and the white ceiling.

"I'm trying out the nerve," he said, as though that meant anything. He reached up to the light over the mirror and he thought the nerve had frayed and split. He imagined a ragged sort of string tied round his spine. "It's more like needles and pins now," he presently said.

"I thought men never had pains," she said. "Only neurotic women." He could not guess the direction of her thoughts, for their knowledge of each other was intimate, not general. "Who gave you the electric toothbrush?" she asked.

"No one. I bought it."

"What did you want a thing like that for?" He realized that she thought she had caught him out and that his wife had given it to him—probably for Father's Day, with a ribbon around it. She was still thin-skinned about his family, even now, after he had proven there was nothing but her. His children were altogether taboo; their very names carried misfortune. Giving her the cards to post—his attempts to bring about a casual order—must have seemed such a violation of safety that she was probably amazed at finding them both here, intact.

He started to answer but the habit of clandestine holidays cut him short, for they heard a high-pitched exchange in English outside the door: "...sent in an unsealed envelope to save sixpence." "I should have torn it up." "So I did."

She smiled at him. The day was still safe; the complicity between them had from the beginning been as important as love.

Of course she needed him, she said to herself. Without him, she would never have known about love, only about gratitude, affection, claustrophobia. She sat on the bed and spread the torn coat on her knee. The lining was rent under the arm; with difficulty she joined the ragged seams. The material seemed stiff and old, and it was unpleasant to handle. Intellectual sweat, she said deep within her mind.

"The first time you saw me with Aunt Freda you said, 'She is using you as a *femme de charme*,' remember? But she had been kind, as always, and she'd bought me a sumptuous velvet skirt and a leather jacket, and I didn't see why I couldn't wear them together. I must have been a sight. I thought all *you* could see were my bitten nails."

"You and your aunt were too tied up," he said. "Too dependent on each other." He sounded as if the aunt were to blame for a flaw in Gitta; at least that was the meaning she selected. She could have straightened out the right and wrong of it, but what would their lives become, with so many explanations? She imagined them, a worn-out old couple in a traveller's climate, not speaking much— explanations having devoured conversation long ago— pretending to be all right when anyone looked at them. "Women are bad for each other," he said. She thought he was describing her life without him, but perhaps it was another woman's—he'd had nothing but daughters. She felt, obscurely, that a searing discussion had taken place.

Settling into an armchair he groaned sincerely. He said, "Well, you liked old Leget. That's a good thing."

She looked up and said simply, "I told you. I worship him. I would do anything he asked."

"Don't ever tell him that."

"I mean it. I worshipped his films before I ever knew you knew him. It's talent I love. I'd do anything."

"So you said. What *has* he asked you to do?"

"It's just one scene, to tell you the truth. I...I sort of sleepwalk through American Express. Don't laugh. *Stop* it! I don't mean walking in my sleep. You know how sometimes you feel no one can see you, because you are so intent—looking for a friend, let's say—and suddenly you wake up and notice everybody staring? I can't explain it the way he does. Actually, I don't need to say anything. I just am. I exist. I'm me, Gitta."

"You aren't you if you don't open your mouth. Also, if you don't talk, it means he pays you a good deal less."

"Don't be so small. You know very well I am paid and how much. It doesn't come out of his pocket. I'm not some little tart he picked up in the Café Select."

"I'm going to be sorry I introduced you to Leget," he said. "You're doting."

"He doesn't care for women," she said primly, and, as if one statement completed the other, "He has his wife."

She wondered if he was trying to tell her she owed him the interview. But she remembered all that she owed him, particularly now, when he had given up everything for her—his children, and the room he was used to working in, and his wife answering the telephone (she could imagine no other use for her), and perhaps his job. He might go into a news agency here, but it was a come-down. That might be the greatest loss of all; it was the only one he mentioned. But she was astute enough at times to guess he might not speak of what bothered him most. How could she match his sacrifice? She had rid herself of everything that might divert a scrap of her love; she had thrown away a small rabbit with nylon fur, a bracelet made of painted wooden links, both highly charged with the powers of fortune. It was not enough; she was frightened without her talismans, and they were still not on an equal footing. She often said to him now, "Never leave me."

She cut off the thread and went on, "Leget is young to be married. I mean, so definitely married."

"There's no age limit." He was not yet divorced. He had jumped without a net—at his time of life! When he had talked gently to her in the old days, at the beginning, it had been about herself. Now, as he composed a new message in which he figured, she heard the word "compulsive" or perhaps it was "impulsive"—she could not take it in. She felt utterly an impostor, sewing for a grown person who ought to look after his own clothes, as if sewing were a translation of devotion. He was unwell, of course, and out of his element. Inactive, he seemed to disappear. We are all selfish, she decided. She had been devoted to her aunt, but selfishness was a green fly, unobserved, the colour of the leaf. She murmured, as she had many times in the past two days, "Don't leave me," but it was only a new exorcism. She had shed her talismans— oh, mistake! If he made love to her, that might be a way out of their predicament; it seemed, in fact, the only way. But when he crept onto the bed, behind her back, it was only because he'd had enough of sitting in the chair.

"I'm not going out," she said suddenly. "Ring downstairs and see if they can send someone out to the café for you."

She turned and saw that he was watching her closely. Just as his hand went to the telephone she said, "Darling, a hideous thing happened today. I didn't tell you. When I was coming home after seeing Leget, the rain started pelting, so I stopped in a doorway, and some man, a sort of working man, was there, in the dark. I had the feeling if I said 'Partez!' he would go, and I was ashamed to think it —to think he was inferior, I mean. All at once he moved between me and the street, and when I looked back I saw the building was empty—it was being torn down from the inside. The outside walls were all that was left. I got my back against the wall, and as he walked toward me I pushed him away with both hands, with all my might. He opened his mouth—it was full of blood. He sort of fell against me; some of it got on my coat. He staggered back and fell in a heap, and I left him. I walked away very slowly to show I wasn't frightened, but I was so upset that I went in a café and had a drink and watched their television for about an hour. I was afraid if I came straight back to you I might be hysterical and it might bother you."

"You probably aren't hungry then, are you?" he asked.

"Of course I'm hungry. I'm as hungry as you are. You know perfectly well I haven't eaten the whole day."

He seemed to take it for granted she was making this up—she could tell. He had known her to do it before, when she was anxious to change the meaning of a situation, but in those days she had been living with her aunt, and trying to make her life seem vivid and interesting to him.

"Why didn't you shout, or call someone?"

"Because I wanted to show him I wasn't afraid of him."

"Weren't you?"

"I wanted to kill him. I was murderous."

"That's understandable," he said. "You'll realize tomorrow, or when you wake up in the night, that you were frightened. What shall I ask them to fetch you from the café? A ham sandwich? Two sandwiches?"

"I don't care." She was bitterly offended, alone, astray, for he was making little of the danger she had been in. All he seemed to have on his mind was food. He spoke into the telephone, explained that he was very ill. Sandwiches, he said, and he knew the French for "corkscrew."

She said, "What if it isn't real? What if I made it up?"

"Even if you have, it's frightened you. You've frightened yourself."

"Aren't you?"

"I wasn't in on it."

"Aren't you frightened that I wanted to kill someone?"

"I haven't got round to that," he said. "If you invented it *only* to frighten me, I'll try to respond."

"All right. I made it up to worry you, let's say. But there's blood on the sleeve of my coat. As for you, you only got this lumbago because you don't want us to be happy. Now that your wife knows, you don't enjoy making love to me."

"Be an angel," he said. "Don't say too much more now."

"As long as Aunt Freda had me," she said, "you had me and all the rest. She kept me for you. And she didn't mind your being married, because it meant I'd never leave her. There, that's what I think. Do you want to go back? Aunt Freda said men never leave home unless their wives are hell."

"My wife wasn't hell."

"Then there's no explanation, is there?"

"There bloody well is, and you know what it is."

"We're like children, aren't we?" she said. "In a way?"

Knowing more than she did about children, he said, sadly, "No, not at all."

She started to answer, "If anything goes wrong now, I suppose I have no one to blame but myself," which came out, without her meaning it that way, "no one to love but myself."

She was frightened, as he had predicted, in the night. She supposed that the man who had come out of the shadows of the courtyard and was now blocking her way to the street intended to kill her. "I don't need to die," she said, meaning that she did not want to be transformed; that life was manageable. He stood with his arms spread, hands dangling, as though imitating a clumsy bird. "Oh, look," she cried. "It isn't fair!," for the bus she wanted

243

slipped away from the curb. No one could see her in here, and there was nothing left of the queue she had abandoned so as to shelter from the rain. "I'm late as it is," she said. It seemed her only grievance.

She supposed he knew no English. "If only I'd said 'Get out' the instant I saw you," she raged at him. "You'd have gone. You'd have respected the tone. All you deserve from me is commands. 'Get out,' I ought to have said. 'Get out!'"

The steps of his curious bird dance brought him near. He stretched his mouth so that she saw the bloody gums. He had been in a fight. She smelled the breath of someone frightened; she saw his eyes. She understood that he had no plans for her: he was drunk and vacant, like her aunt. She remembered the subdual of drinks, the easy victories. "I'm going out that door!" she said. Her triumphs over her aunt had been of this order. Feelings about other people she had never specifically understood sent her toward him—into his arms, he might have thought. He was afflicted with the worst of curses—obscurity, a life without meaning—while she would never be forgotten, unless she let some fool destroy her. When they were almost as close as lovers she pushed him away, one hand on the other and both on his throat. He should have fallen back and cracked his head and made an end to it, but instead he knelt, sagged; his face, in passing, knocked against the sleeve of her coat. "Oh, you'll be all right," she said. She spoke in the *jeune Anglaise* voice she had only that day been advised to lose.

"Partez," she said softly in the dark, and again, a little louder, *"Partez!"* and then, as he began to come awake, "Would you be very unhappy? Would you miss me? Is it true you don't believe a word I say?"

GOOD DEED

❖

HOUSES of widows on the French Riviera have in common the outsize pattern of flowers on the chintzes; there is too much furniture everywhere, most of it larger than life. The visitor feels, as he is intended to, very small. These are child's-view houses, though real children may feel oppressed in them, and are not often welcome to stay. The photographs jostling each other on tables are of grown, formidable people—sepia-tinted parents in profile, brothers dressed for old wars. All are dead now. The most recent pictures are likely to be of animals; inquiring, the visitor learns they have died too. In the kitchen, where a slut in felt slippers has been taught to make treacle pudding, the food on the shelves gratifies, at last, a nursery craving for sweets. There is jam and honey and golden syrup, and condensed milk that can be poured over or stirred into nearly everything. Left to herself, with the possiblity of having life as she now wants it, the solitary old woman recovers a child's dream diet, a child's pet animals; she furnishes a vast drawing room intended for giants, and creates her mother's bedroom, as she remembers it—bright and secret, with smooth curtains, and cats all over the bed.

The room in which Olivia now waited for her guest to arrive contained, along with a tribe of animals, a moth-eaten shako hung on a nail, a regimental drum, a parrot cage with nothing inside it, and the picture of a baby boy or girl, perfectly bald, upon a cushion. Although she was naturally idle, waiting for anyone tried her nerves. She began, in her mind, a letter saying, "My dear Hugo, It is three o'clock, and there is no sign of your secretary. I am afraid the poor creature has perished. The plane that was bringing her from London was seen punctually descending upon Nice Airport, when suddenly it exploded and shot, flaming, into the sea. Old Joseph, who was standing beside his taxi holding a cardboard sign with Miss Freeman's name printed on it, heard the screams of young women (your secretary's certainly among them) above the roar and hiss of the flames as the plane met the waves. I am most frightfully sorry about your having lost Miss Freeman, and do hope you find another secretary soon."

In reality it was only half past two, which still left a margin of time for Miss Freeman's destruction. Olivia now began to revise the instructions she had drawn up for the disposal of her own body after her death. She wished to be cremated, which would cause one great and final inconvenience. She was certain to die where she lived, on the coast below Nice; which meant that the person chosen by Olivia would be obliged to accompany her coffin to Marseille and, as recommended by a curious French law, identify her once before she was rendered unrecognizable. She thought of every grotesque possibility, including that of a real mistake, and added to the list of victims the name of Hugo Mellett. Hugo was quite far down on the list. First (and he would certainly be the first refusal) came her brother-in-law, who was a Greek living in Athens, and who had never been able to bear the sight of Olivia in life. Next came old Joseph, who had once been her chauffeur, and now drove a taxi. A habit of slavishness might bind Joseph to commands from beyond the grave; he was dutiful in his behaviour but stealthy with regard to his own feelings. Olivia had called him a coolie to his face, and his face had not changed. For many years she had been trying to give old Joseph a shock; she could think of no greater shock for him than the sight of his former employer going up in flames. She added to her instructions, "I want this treated as a pagan ceremony," for Joseph was an unquestioning Roman Catholic.

Just after three o'clock she heard his old green Daimler creeping along the drive. Miss Freeman had evidently caught the right plane, which was clever of someone who had been described to Olivia as not quite right in the head. Olivia then heard the bell, the door, the car starting up again, and finally a sound that was still absolutely excruciating to her, though she had left Ireland some sixty years before: an English female voice. The pitch of Miss Freeman's voice was an octave higher than it need have been, as if a penny whistle were lodged in her throat. The clock in Olivia's room chimed the quarter hour, which made Olivia grumble, "What a lot of noise, and she's only just got here."

Miss Freeman had been admitted by Olivia's latest kitchen slattern, who climbed the stairs silently to announce the guest. Olivia placed a long finger against her lips. The cook shrugged; she was here only because she would put up with the cats, and understood English. Madame was resting but would shortly put her clothes on, Miss Freeman was told. An hour later the cook came up again and stood looking at Olivia. "What am I to say to her now?" she said. "That Madame is fully dressed and playing with her cats?"

"Give the creature tea."

"She prefers to wait for Madame."

"Isn't there a newspaper she can read? She could go for a good walk. That's it—tell her to go for a walk."

There were no walks—none, at least, Miss Freeman could know about. Olivia's house backed on a highway clogged with cars. Moreover, if what Olivia had heard of Miss Freeman was true, she would never be brave enough to venture out alone in a strange place.

Miss Freeman belonged to Hugo Mellett; Olivia imagined her made up from one of Hugo's ribs. Hugo and Olivia maintained a light ironic correspondence, in which Hugo revealed a good deal of himself. He trusted Olivia completely. He had not seen her for twenty years now, but she remained in his mind as the beautiful elderly widow who had once shown him uncommon understanding.

"Wendy Freeman is a first-rate secretary," he had written. "Try to find out what has gone wrong. It might be overwork, but this office is better designed and infinitely more pleasant than her own home. As her breakdown was set off by the sight of an electronic machine, I should keep all mechanical objects out of her way. It happened when she saw a computer. What do you imagine the poor child had expected to see?"

"Now, *that* is a *brain*," Hugo had said of the computer.

"It is larger than I had thought," Wendy Freeman had remarked. "But it can't be a brain, because it has nothing but memory. It has no feelings. It can't even change its mind."

"That is the best part about it," Hugo had replied. "It can do a job without steaming up the atmosphere." It was known to Hugo that computers were capable of violent and unreasonable behaviour, of hysteria even, but he did not tell his secretary this, for he did not wish her to follow suit. She had been tearful and jumpy recently, and this visit to a display of electronic machines was Hugo's attempt to distract and cheer her up. He was an architectural engineer consulted on large housing projects. He had worked in Zurich in the 1930s, and in Milan after the last war. He knew to the cubic centimetre the amount of space into which a family may be compressed without incidence of paranoia; he knew when to allow half an inch lift to a ceiling and when to be firm.

"What an ass you are," Wendy said, staring at the computer. He pretended not to hear. Breakdowns in machines and in persons seldom occur without warning. He felt responsible.

"I should like to send you to an old friend of mine in a warm climate," he said. "She is a marvellous person." Wendy's eyelids turned pink. He pretended not to see.

"You are generous," she said, a week later, as he drove her to a place unpropitious to outbursts of any kind— the London airport. He was not unaware of Wendy, and, as he was something of a hypochondriac, often wished he had someone to look after him; but he thought he was too old for Wendy, and he had been married twice.

"I expect I *am* generous," he said.

"And kind," Wendy went on bitterly.

"That too." He did not think of it as flattery on her part, or conceit on his own. Who should know Hugo better than these two, his secretary and himself?

If he had known at this moment how Wendy was cooling her heels in a decayed drawing room, sitting on the edge of an armchair that had been clawed by cats, staring, terrified, at the monstrous cat on the mantelpiece that seemed about to spring at her face, he would not have thought Olivia rude. Olivia, when younger, had kept people waiting for hours, and they had always come back. The attraction women exert lies often in what has been said about them. Her lovers were a legend, her women friends faithful, and her husband had worshipped her. Hugo had heard him described as a funny, ugly little Greek. The Greek admired her because she was blue-eyed and fair, and he thought her an intellectual—something he would not have tolerated in a woman from his own country. It was true that she had a reputation for cleverness. She had, at the age of twenty, written a spiteful novel about her Irish relations, cutting herself off from them forever but gaining a lively existence based on a

rumor of past performances; for no one remembered exactly what it was she had done. The Greek died, before the
clumsy villas they had lived in along the coast became
old-fashioned and were torn down. The books he had
amassed for his wife, thinking she read them, became
speckled and brown. After his death Olivia discovered he
considered her cold and brainless and a fraud. She was
shown a copy of a letter he had sent his brother in Athens.
"They love and pursue her *because* she is made of marble,"
he said. "If I live long enough, I may understand." He
made his brother his heir, which was, she thought, a
trivial way of showing dissatisfaction. This house, which
was Olivia's for her lifetime, reverted to the brother-in-
law at her death. He was eighty-one, but he wished to
outlive her so that he could demolish the villa and put up
a garage and filling station in its place; he had said so.

Hugo came to Olivia at a time of great crisis in his life.
He sat at her feet, wondered if he was in love with her,
and unburdened himself of secrets that were no one's
business but his. It was, for him, unforgettable; he
supposed he and Olivia were now tied for life. She was
old enough to be his mother; would she claim him
forever? It turned out that she did not want to. For years,
remembering her, he praised her composure and her
disinterested replies. She never judged me, he believed.
But her calmness was only because she had heard anguish
before. Questions such as "What am I to do? What will
become of me?," which one might hear in the course of a
close friendship, in an atmosphere of stress, were Olivia's
small talk. As her husband had observed, her fascination
resided in her failings. People were drawn by her cyni-
cism and selfishness; by her known preference for animals over people; by her cruel theories about her friends
and her indifference to their fate. She heard, with self-
possession, the usual questions: "Where did I go wrong?

Was there one first mistake? Am I repeating a pattern? Is the failure in my character, or have I been unlucky?" She sat, hands folded, only the pressure of one thumb on the other betraying a brief impatience. Hugo had thought, she despises everyone except me. He had not sought a warm listener, for warm people are not exclusive: they are kind about everything. He had looked for, and found, the concentration that could be obtained only from someone entirely idle, with a shrewd eye, a selective ear and a spirit of flint.

"There is nothing whatever the matter," Olivia had said, slowly. "You are thoroughly selfish, Hugo, and that's all. You've got enough to live on?" It was the only problem she took to heart—that and one's health. ("A pain? Where, right side or left? Before or after your food? I have seen people carried off in twenty-four hours.") She had no qualms about saying it, and no one had ever minded being told. Hugo was relieved; believing himself exploited and indecisive, it was a deliverance to be thought selfish and headstrong. The threat of a fatal illness froze his terrors into a single shape. He was completely demented when he left her, but cured of his immediate torments. This was more than twenty years in the past, and blurred at the edges. He said to Wendy, "I am sending you to someone very kind."

Olivia did not come down; Wendy was summoned upstairs. She found her hostess wearing a crêpe de Chine dress that reminded Wendy of old films in which the heroine has curly blond hair. Wendy still wore the clothes she had put on that morning. Hugo and the airport seemed weeks ago. She felt in exile. The cook had lied about having offered tea; and no one had asked her if she wanted to wash her hands. She sat on the edge of Olivia's bed and became homesick.

Olivia's first question was "How did you like old Joseph? I am speaking of your taxi-driver."

"He had a sign with my name," said Wendy. "I thought that was intelligent of him. We didn't speak much, though he does know English."

"Hugo said it was best not to have you paged at the airport," said Olivia. "A mechanical system."

Wendy did not respond; she seemed in fact puzzled.

"Hugo thinks you are overworked," Olivia continued.

Wendy submissively stroked the cat that was trying to take possession of her part of the bed. Her obsession was Hugo Mellett. She was putting her faith once and for all in Hugo's magic friend. She would have lighted a candle before Olivia's effigy if she had thought it would do any good. She was an eager but careful girl; she felt she had been too careful until now. She did not mind how many times he had been married. She saw Olivia's long hands, and wild white hair. Wendy believed in the solidarity of women and thought her youth would render her appealing to Olivia. She looked straight into the old woman's eyes, in the mirror.

Olivia had fallen asleep; she often slept with her eyes open now. In a brief dream she saw old Joseph, who, after having been chauffeur to this lady and that, had kept the habit of driving at thirty miles an hour in the stately car someone had let him buy on easy terms after sixteen years of service. It still resembled a private car, with fresh flowers in containers, and the folded rug on the seat. No one had ever been so docile; as pleased with little. Olivia awoke and began rattling rings and pins in a china dish on her dressing table. "Sapphires would look well on you," she said, as though there had never been an interruption. How long had Wendy been in her room —hours? Days? "They are mine, but promised to my niece, who is a fat bore." She spoke rapidly and did not address her remarks to Wendy. "Are you superstitious? Some women are, about opals. These would suit you, but they belonged to Nicky's mother and must go to his brother in Athens after I die. He is dull, and so is his wife. Most people are dull dogs, when it comes to that. I feel it most keenly about the Greeks, though I have never set foot in the country. When my sister-in-law came here from Athens on a visit, she put on sparklers every night, but I made her sit down to a poached egg on toast. 'That is my supper,' I told her. 'Cutlet or egg, and that is that.' If I went to Athens I would eat slops without complaining. I told her that too."

"What a dear little girl," said Wendy, of the bald baby. She had not been able to follow anything of Olivia's explanation. "Is it you?"

"My son," said Olivia. "Just as he was becoming interesting to me he had a sort of fit and died. If he were still living, he would be older than Hugo."

Wendy, watching closely to see that Olivia was not looking at her, put down the cat. She had been prepared to accept everything about Hugo, and had swallowed whole the assumption that understatement was the mark of a delicate mind. Hugo might have said exactly the same thing, in the same negligent tone: "had a sort of fit and died." She was determined to save Hugo, and hoped she had not been born too late.

Wendy was not forthcoming about her problems, and before the end of her stay, which was seven days long, Olivia was sick of having her about. The girl's eager face when she came down to lunch put her off for the rest of the day. "You don't want to talk to an old thing like me," she said, knocking the cane on the floor to summon the cats for their meal. She made as much noise as she could.

"Oh but I do," said Wendy. "Because that's what I'm here for."

Exasperated, Olivia suddenly leaned on the cane. She seemed so disjointed and helpless that Wendy rushed forward, thinking Olivia had doubled over and could not straighten up — which was in fact what had happened.

"I am all right," said Olivia. "I find the position restful. My dear, why don't you marry some young man instead of wasting your time with old people? You have cried every night — your eyelids are like fuchsias."

"I am in love with someone who never looks at me," Wendy muttered. That was her secret, her neurotic confession. Olivia, having straightened up without help, was tempted to slap her. She thought, with nostalgia, of the old days, when one could get rid of a dull guest by sending him down the coast to Rapallo with a letter of introduction, or up the other way to Mr Maugham. How dare Hugo send me this, she thought.

Wendy repeated her charge that some man or other never looked at her.

"Forget about him. Marry someone."

"I can't. I see him every day. He is the one I love."

"Love?" said Olivia. "What you need is eighteen months' travel and some decent dresses."

"You must have loved your husband," said Wendy, controlling herself. She knew, and minded, about her eyelids colouring. Her sandy lashes darkened after only a few tears.

"I don't know about that," said Olivia. "I wanted to get out of Ireland. Has Hugo ever tried to make love to you?"

"No," said Wendy. "No, he has not."

Olivia, having cut her poached egg up with a spoon, put the plate on the floor for one of the cats. "Are you sure he likes it?" Wendy had asked the first time she saw this. "No, he never touches it," Olivia replied. "But, you see, he is so terribly fond of me." With a little shudder, Wendy now averted her eyes. Not knowing what Olivia was talking about was no help at all; it simply made her feel she had been put down a well.

Olivia said, "Secretaries know everything about the men who employ them, isn't that so? Hugo was a dedicated homosexual until the age of twenty-seven, when he married a woman for her money. Ianthe was her name. She died of drink in a hotel room in Geneva, and he then married a crony of hers, whose hair was purple and who wore garnets on a dried or non-existing bosom. They paraded their squalid alliance up and down this very coast, and then she died. He neglected her shamefully in her last illness, and after a short period of neutrality began having — as a sort of pre-senility, I suppose — affairs with young females."

Wendy listened with her head bent and her lips apart. Then she said, "I doubt if he has lived on anyone's money. He has practised his profession all his life. I once had to catalogue his published articles — I don't know of any gaps. I don't gossip or listen to gossip." She had been quite brave, but now she choked.

To stop any sign of tears, which she could not countenance, Olivia produced one of her eternity games, with which she had often sent her true neurotics home for a sleepless night. She omitted the simplest question, "Would you prefer, for eternity, to be shut up in a cloistered nunnery or an Oriental bordel?," knowing the innocent and devoted girl would jump at the bordel, thinking that that was where she could do the most good. "I wonder...I know so little about young people now," Olivia said. "Which would you choose for eternity? Now, do think carefully. A cell crowded with filthy and ignorant prisoners, or a charming house and garden provided with every mortal comfort except a human presence?"

"Why, the cell full of people, of course," said Wendy. She spoke with composure, and even some surprise.

"It is forever," said Olivia. "And their habits are disgusting."

"So are people's minds," said Wendy. "Even when their manners seem perfect. Habits can be broken."

"They are unteachable. You would never have a second's privacy again."

"I wouldn't try to teach them all. I would take one, and teach him. The only privacy you can have in real life is invented anyway." She had just experienced the greatest fright she had ever thought possible: she had seen an infinity of silence and light, millions of silent perfect meals, silent aimless walks in a garden where the sky was a witness but would never speak.

"You say 'him' as if he existed," Olivia said. "You are not playing the game. He would never understand a word you were saying. He would laugh at you."

Wendy did look then, not at Olivia but at the door left open for the cats. "I wonder if in eternity there would be no such thing as corruption anymore. How do we know there aren't planets where everything we think right is forbidden, and what seems decent to us revolting to them?"

Olivia said, to the girl who had broken down over an electronic machine, "You aren't afraid of dying, then?" Wendy did not reply, and presently Olivia went on, "I think Hugo ought to marry you."

"Why?" said Wendy. "He won't think of it, and if he asked me now I would refuse. I'm speaking the truth." She felt baited beyond endurance, and could only lie with all her heart. "If he asked me, I would say no."

Eternity has done it, Olivia decided. She will see everything as solitude or a cell.

She wrote that day to her old friend, "You must ask this girl to marry you. She could be your salvation. She is quite sensible, but madly in love with you, and would accept in a minute. Tell her it is forever — that you have thought it over carefully." Believing that both his previous wives must have proposed to him, she added, "Take her out and feed her and get a very good bottle of wine." She had a shadowy desire to punish Hugo for having foisted on her this dull girl, but there was a nagging irritation too. For twenty years, and without her ever having to see him, she had remained the only woman in his life. He had never bothered about the health or the feelings of anyone, until Wendy. If he believed her letter but did not wish to marry Wendy — if, indeed, the very idea was abominable to him — he would feel uncomfortable keeping Wendy in his office. If she refused him, he would be humiliated. If she accepted, he would soon learn he was in a cell with an ardent educator, and fly to Olivia for counsel.

After posting the letter, Olivia accompanied Wendy to the airport. She could scarcely conceal her excitement that the girl was leaving.

"Joseph was the best chauffeur on the coast years ago," she said, loudly, as she sat in the back of his car with Wendy. "But he drove terrible women....Joseph! Who was it wouldn't let anyone eat oranges because if she smelled oranges she would be sure they had been stolen from her trees?"

"Mrs Willcox, Madame," he said, without turning.

"And smoking — who wouldn't allow the smell of it anywhere?"

"Many ladies, Madame. Nearly every one."

Wendy said only, "There is nothing like that now."

Olivia smiled. "Who was the one with the riding crop, Joseph?" she called again.

His eyes, seen in the mirror, did not change. They crept along the Corniche road with a streamer of cars behind. He seemed to be considering something outside himself.

"Madame is thinking of my next-to-last employer," he said.

"So I am! She had a riding crop or a little belt—am I right, Joseph?—and when he drove too fast or too slowly or hadn't stopped where she wanted because of some silly rule, she would beat him about the shoulders. She was a sight! He put up with it. It might have been a fly. Oh, he was used to it, of course." And so she saw Wendy off.

Hugo's telegram arrived seven days later. It said, "DONE AND DONE A THOUSAND THANKS." Wendy had accepted! If Olivia had stopped to think of the sound of "a thousand thanks," she would have been struck by its finality. A language softer than English might leave room for an answer, but the double "th" was barbed wire. *Done, a thousand thanks....* Why, she thought, it was the lightest kind of gratitude. It applied to a pleasant luncheon party or a box of *marrons glacés* or a month-old copy of the *Observer* containing some outrage. Hugo might have wired exactly the same message if she had advised him to have a tooth pulled and supplied the name of her dentist. She wrote, "Hugo, do not marry this girl. We are both mistaken about her, you in thinking she was insane, and I in believing she was too innocent. She is a liar, and as hard as nails. *Do* consider this letter, for I think the warning I am sending you may be my one good deed. Miss Freeman butters her bread and cuts it into little squares. She spends half the day looking for her comb. She only pretends to listen. She will drive you mad."

They came south for their honeymoon, and on their way home stopped overnight at a hotel near Olivia's house. The bride had brought a tin of Jackson's Earl Grey tea for Olivia, and a family of rubber mice for the cats. They did not call on Olivia but asked her to come and see them. She was so astonished at being summoned that she went. She was kept waiting in their sitting room. She sat fully six minutes, depositing cat hair on a blue velvet *bergère*. Wendy came in, blooming, in command and looking some fifteen years older. Her hair was cut straight across her brow, and she had added a false chignon.

"I think Hugo may have had a mild form of sunstroke," said Wendy in a low voice. "You will see that one of his eyes is quite bloodshot."

"It was always his weak point," said Olivia. "Reckless exposure. What is that sound?"

"Hugo's electric razor."

"Poor man!" said Olivia, meaning how unfortunate, what a comedown, what a miserable link with the world of ordinary men. Hugo *was* bloodshot, but younger. The two had conspired, in a short time, to arrive at an average age of about thirty-seven.

"Come along, Hugo," said Olivia. "I'm giving you lunch. No intellectual conversation, now. I want to hear something interesting."

Hugo replied, "What's the food going to be like?"

Wendy said patiently, "It's too late for lunch, darling. It's nearly supper-time, and we shall have that on the train."

"We were remembering Olivia's famous luncheons," he said, and turned slightly away from her, as if he did not wish to be overtaken by the memory.

"They really consisted of bringing together people who could not possibly like one another, and letting them try to get the better in conversation until the wine made them all too stupid to talk," said Olivia. "But sometimes I took my party to a restaurant. I would decide the menu for everyone in advance. I took it for granted they all went out to be nourished. Would a sane person desert his own table for any other reason?"

Hugo looked confused, as if time were tangled in his mind, and Wendy said, "I'm afraid he must rest until train time. By the way, do you think Joseph would drive us?"

"A good deed in a naughty world, or something of the kind," said Olivia, rising. But Hugo seemed to have forgotten what she meant.

They strolled, following the porter, up to the end of the platform. When the train swept in, she remembered having read in her girlhood a warning that the vacuum created when air was displaced by an onrushing express, or even the giddiness caused by the sight of the wheels, could make one lose consciousness. In her mind was a traveller, surrounded by alps of luggage, including a bird in a cage; the traveller stepped back from the train, an example of prudence. She stepped back and nearly fell. Wendy was reading the numbers on the carriages as the express slowed.

"Seven, that's ours." With dumb show she indicated the carriage to the porter. Seeing his wife walking away with the porter, Hugo rose from the bench where he had been resting. He trusted Wendy to attend to everything, and to come back for him. The porter was handing their luggage in through the window to the sleeping-car attendant. Wendy, having set this in motion, took his arm. "The train only stops a minute," she threw over her shoulder. Olivia, who had established long ago that she disliked being kissed, wondered why neither of them kissed her. From the window of their compartment they looked down — first Wendy, who said something and smiled and urged Hugo to stand up and say a word to his old friend, who was on the platform.

"Hugo," Olivia said loudly, leaning on her cane and looking up at him. "I am very ill." His eyes expressed mild distress, perhaps about the train, which had begun to roll slowly. They were borne apart. She felt as if she were sliding and unable to stop herself. She said, over considerable noise, "Pain in my ribs, just below the shoulder, on the left side." Hugo smiled anxiously. "My brother-in-law is going to sell my house. Do you hear me? It is in his name. He can do whatever he likes with it. What shall I do? When they visited me from Greece"—her voice rose—"my sister-in-law tried to throw me down the stairs. The cats have taken over the house. I am afraid of them. Someone ought to protect me from the cats. One sits on my chest in the night, and when I try to move..."

"Goodbye, Olivia," said her old friend. She saw the words take form and float. He leaned out of the window. Beyond the station the train bent round a curve, and now a hand with a fluttering handkerchief replaced Hugo's bowing form.

Hugo is deaf as a post, Olivia decided, walking away. I hope he will not send me any more of his friends.

"Joseph!" she said. "What would you do if I were to die? Would you look after my funeral?"

She sat in the middle of the back seat, and Joseph drove at a snail's pace, taking no notice of the furious drivers behind. "Answer me!" she said. "Would you adopt all my cats?" His head, his neck, his hands on the wheel seemed acquiescent. What a coolie he was! He had the soul of a carpet. "Why don't you answer?" she said. "I know *you* aren't deaf."

"I would do whatever was correct," he said. That was all.

If she had had a riding crop, a belt with a buckle, she would have struck him. His head turned an inch, then another; for a second his eyes left the road, but his expression was as she had always known it.

What a terrible face he must have when he is not with me, she thought. "Joseph!" she said. "Do you think I am dangerous and old?"